DANGEROUS REALITY

malorie
blackman

CORGI BOOKS

DANGEROUS REALITY
A CORGI BOOK 978 0 552 55167 0

First published in Great Britain by Doubleday,
an imprint of Random House Children's Publishers UK
A Random House Group Company

Doubleday edition published 1999
Corgi edition published 2000
Corgi edition reissued 2004

This edition published 2012

19

Set in Bembo

Corgi Books are published by Random House Children's Publishers UK,
61–63 Uxbridge Road, London W5 5SA

www.**randomhouse**.co.uk
www.**randomhousechildrens**.co.uk
www.**totallyrandombooks**.co.uk

Addresses for companies within The Random House Group Limited can be found at:
www.randomhouse.co.uk/offices.htm

THE RANDOM HOUSE GROUP Limited Reg. No. 954009

A CIP catalogue record for this book is available from the British Library.

Penguin Random House is committed to a sustainable future for
our business, our readers and our planet. This book is made from
Forest Stewardship Council® certified paper.

MIX
Paper from
responsible sources
FSC® C018179

Printed and bound in Great Britain by Clays Ltd, Elcograf S.p.A.

For Neil and Lizzy,
with love

Chapter One

How it Started!

Hi! I'm Dominic. Dominic Painter. And, yes, that really is my name. And, no, I'm not making it up. And yes, I have heard the one about the painter, the decorator and the window cleaner! Now that that's out of the way, I want to tell you about my mum. My mum is Carol Painter. Have you heard of her? You haven't? Where have you been? Living on Mars? I thought everyone had heard of my mum. Well, it's like this, my mum makes things. I don't mean things! I mean THINGS – in great, big, screaming capital letters. And her latest wonder is VIMS, which stands for the Virtual Interactive Mobile System. You've never heard of that either? OK, then. Sit back, relax and I'll tell you all about it. This is the story of Mum's latest miracle – VIMS – and how it almost got me killed.

Chapter Two

Marriage!

'Dominic, I want you to sit down.'

'I am sitting down, Mum.' I looked from Mum to Jack and back again. They both stood in front of me with fixed smiles and anxious eyes.

'Dominic, we've got something to tell you.'

That much I'd worked out for myself. 'Yes, Mum?'

I watched as, without looking down, Mum fumbled around for and found Jack's hand. And then I knew what was coming.

'Is Jack going to move in with us?' I asked.

'Well, your mum and I thought we'd do it the other way around. You two will move in with me,' smiled Jack.

'Are you two going to live together?'

'Us three are going to live together,' Jack stressed, the easy smile still on his face.

'And when is all this meant to happen?'

Mum and Jack looked at each other for silent confirmation. 'We thought we'd get married at the end of November, so we'd all be together for Christmas,' said Mum.

'You're getting married?' I stood up slowly.

'Yes, of course. What did you think we were talking about?' Mum frowned.

What happened next was really mean. I know I shouldn't have done it, but I couldn't help it. I really couldn't.

'You're joking, right? You're not *really* going to marry Jack, are you?'

'Dominic, you like Jack,' Mum said, surprised. 'And you're always saying . . .'

'I don't like Jack. I hate him.' I glared at him. The look on his face almost made me give myself away there and then. 'I hate him. He's not part of this family and he never will be.'

'Dominic, please,' Mum pleaded, appalled. Whatever else she'd expected, she certainly hadn't expected this reaction from me.

I looked from Mum to Jack. He looked stunned. I glared at him and watched as moments later his expression cleared. And then I knew he had caught on. He stepped forward, his expression deadly serious.

'Now wait just a minute, Dominic . . .' he began.

'No, you wait just a minute, maggot-features!'

'Don't call me that, you grotty little oik!'

'Jack! Dominic, apologize at once.' Mum didn't know who to round on first.

'Apologize to a rhino's bum like him? No way!'

'Now wait just a minute, you . . . you . . .' And then Jack went and spoilt it all by bursting out laughing. And of course, once he'd started, he set me off as well.

'Jack, how could you?!' I said, cracking up. 'We could've wound up Mum for at least another five minutes if you hadn't burst out laughing.'

'What?' Mum still didn't have a clue what was going on.

'I couldn't help it,' Jack replied, actually coughing from laughing so much. 'The look on your mum's face was priceless.'

'You mean, you two didn't mean all that?' Mum said sombrely.

Something in her voice made Jack shut up immediately, and I wasn't too far behind.

'It was just a joke, darling,' Jack tried.

Mum directed a look at him that would have shrivelled a diamond.

'Mum, where's your sense of humour?' I asked.

'You . . . you . . . both of you . . .' Mum spluttered.

Jack pulled Mum into his arms for a tight cuddle. With her head safely on his shoulder, Jack tried to wave me out of the living room but I refused to budge.

'I knew you two were going to tie the knot,' I told

Mum. 'You've been making cow eyes at each other for the last year. And you're always kissing and cuddling. If you knew how embarrassing it looks for two old people like you to be doing that kind of thing, then I'm sure you wouldn't do it! Mind you, Liam says that when you get married all that kissing and cuddling stuff you do will stop – so at least that's something.'

'Who are you calling old?' Jack said indignantly. 'Bloomin' cheek!'

'And what d'you mean "when we get married it'll all stop"?' Mum pulled away from Jack to ask.

'Liam says that married people stop all that mushy stuff once they tie the knot, so the sooner you get married, the better as far as I'm concerned. Then you two can stop showing me up!'

'And just where does Liam get his ideas about married people?' Jack frowned.

'Oh, Liam knows all about these things. He's got cable telly in his room,' I informed him.

'Liam's mum and dad should know better,' Mum said, annoyed. 'And for your information, I don't intend to stop kissing and cuddling Jack until I'm cold in my grave.'

I beamed at her, knowing I'd got her again, although this time I hadn't made it up. Liam really had said that about married people. I looked at Mum and Jack who stood together, still holding hands. They really were too soppy for words. But to tell the truth I was glad Mum was marrying Jack. I liked him very much. Look at the way he'd picked up on the fact that I was just winding up Mum and joined in with me – before he'd given the game away by creasing!

'Congratulations!' I grinned at them.

And suddenly I couldn't stop smiling. I'd spent so long hoping that Mum and Jack would get together and now it was actually going to happen. Mum and Jack made a good couple. What I mean by that is, Mum takes herself far too seriously. She's not so bad now, but you should've seen her before she started going out with Jack two years ago. She has what she calls her funny moments and her serious half-hours! I call them her funny moments and her serious half-years! Mum and Jack have known each other off and on for about ten years now. They both used to work at BFC Power – the huge power plant outside our town that provides power for the entire South West region. Have you seen it? It's a real eyesore. It's that horrible set of huge buildings near the motorway. Mum liked it there though. She said it was the people rather than the place that kept her there for so long.

Everyone used to call Mum, Jack and this other guy called Rayner, the Three Musketeers! They were all good friends. Still are! Rayner still works at BFC but Mum left the power plant nine years ago to work at

Desica International. Jack left BFC five years ago to start working for Mum. But it was only after Jack had been working for Mum for three years that they started going out together. Physically they look totally different. Mum is short and what she calls cuddly. And Jack is tall and thin like a record-breakingly long twig. I call him the world's largest stick insect. And speaking of his name . . .

'What do I call you? Jack or . . . Dad, or what?'

'What d'you want to call me?' Jack asked.

I considered. 'I'll call you Jack.'

'Dominic, don't you think . . . ?' Mum began.

'No. Jack is fine,' Jack interrupted.

Mum looked at Jack and nodded slowly. 'OK. Jack it is, then.'

See what I mean about Mum mellowing out with Jack around? I was looking forward to all three of us being a family. In fact, to be honest, I felt like we were already a family. I couldn't really remember what it was like without Jack. And then a dark grey cloud came scurrying across my blue sky.

'Jack, what about your first wife?' I asked.

'Alison?' Mum answered before Jack could. 'What's Alison got to do with this?'

I suppose I shouldn't have said anything. Mum had told me about Alison in strict confidence but I just wanted to know how things stood.

'Suppose she comes back and . . . and wants you two to get back together?'

'She won't,' said Jack.

'But suppose . . .'

'Dominic, you worry too much. My divorce from Alison came through years ago. She's happy and settled somewhere in Australia and she has no intention of coming back to this country.'

'But suppose . . .'

'Dominic, she's not coming back. Trust me,' Jack said gently.

'OK.' And I did trust him. It's just that I didn't want anything to spoil Mum's and Jack's happiness. Mum had told me how unhappy Jack and Alison had been together and how his wife loved to make Jack's life a misery. Alison had left Jack eight years ago while he was still working at the power plant and he hadn't heard a word from her since. I just didn't want her turning up now and putting a spanner in the works. Mum and Jack were both watching me intently. Not wanting to put a damper on their big 'surprise', I forced my worries out of my head.

'So when are we going to have our dinner?' I asked. 'I'm starving.'

'I should send you to your room for the rest of the night without a bite to eat for that little stunt earlier,' Mum sniffed. 'You really had me going!'

'Mum, that was the idea.' I smiled.

Slowly she smiled back. 'Dominic, you had better watch that peculiar sense of humour you've got there. It could get you into trouble.'

I just grinned at her. 'So what's for dinner then? Feed me. I'm a growing boy.'

'How about we phone for a take-away pizza?' Jack suggested.

'Yeah, OK!' I said, snatching his hand off. I was just about to tell him what I wanted when the phone rang. Mum went to answer it.

'Hello . . . Oh, hello, Rayner.' Mum put her hand over the mouthpiece. 'It's Rayner,' she whispered, as if we hadn't already gathered that. 'What's that? . . . I'm not sure . . . Yes, I know I said . . . OK, OK! . . . No, not tomorrow morning, I'm giving a demo to some suits and uniforms . . . Can't it wait until next week . . . ? Oh, I see . . . OK then, tomorrow afternoon it is. Yes . . . Yes, I said so, didn't I?' Mum looked over at us and raised exasperated eyebrows. 'All right, I'll see you tomorrow. Yes . . . You're welcome. No, I don't – and why d'you always ask me that? Say hello to Monica for me. Bye!'

Mum and Jack exchanged a look.

'He asked you to come back to work at the power plant, didn't he?' Jack said drily.

'Yeah, as always,' Mum sighed.

'I thought so from that emphatic "No, I don't!"' Jack nodded. 'What was the rest of the conversation about?'

'D'you remember when we had dinner with Rayner and Monica a couple of weeks ago and he was talking about the problems they've been having at the power plant? Well, he's still having trouble with a section of their underground pipes and, as it would cost a fortune to dig down and try to find the problem, it occurred to me to suggest he use the VIMS unit to go through the tunnels. I'm sure it wouldn't take VIMS long to find out what's wrong.'

'They've got their own machinery to sort out problems in their pipes,' frowned Jack.

'Yes, I know. But their devices can't seem to find out what's the matter.' Mum shrugged. 'Anyway, it'll be a good road test for the VIMS unit.'

'Which section?' asked Jack.

'Pardon?'

'Which section of the plant has the problem?'

Mum frowned at him. 'I can't remember. A-17? A-19? Something like that.'

'I see.' Jack said the words so quietly, it was a strain to hear them. He had a sombre, thoughtful look on his face. I could almost see the wheels going round in his head.

'Besides, does it matter?' asked Mum.

'No, I guess not,' Jack said seriously. 'But Carol,

I'd be lying if I said I thought this was a good idea.'

'Why not?'

'VIMS needs a lot more testing before we submit it for such a serious workout. Suppose something goes wrong when the VIMS unit is so far underground? How would we get it back?'

'But with all the safeties and backup systems we have in the unit, what could possibly go wrong?' asked Mum.

'Carol, I really don't think we should do this. I think it's more than a little premature.'

'I don't,' Mum argued. 'Besides, I promised Rayner that we'd help him.'

'Then just unpromise him.'

'Why are you so against the idea?' Mum frowned.

Me? I was watching Mum and Jack argue, my head moving from side to side like a spectator at a tennis match.

'What happens if VIMS doesn't work or worse still it works in a way we haven't anticipated?'

'What? For goodness' sake, Jack! VIMS will go down into the section of pipework that has the problem, it will wander up and down the pipes for a while taking photos and sending data back to our remote viewer and if it's a cracked pipe then VIMS may even be able to fix it. What's the big deal?'

'What about our demo tomorrow morning?' Jack said quietly.

'Oh, that!' Mum dismissed with a wave of her hand. 'The demo will be a doddle. We'll show off VIMS to the suits and uniforms, they'll fork over more money for further research and development and we'll still have time to load up the VIMS unit in the afternoon and take it over to Rayner at the power plant.'

'Mum, who are the suits and uniforms you keep talking about?' I couldn't help asking.

'Huh? Oh, that's what I call business people and the military,' Mum explained.

'VIMS isn't going to be used to hurt people, is it?' I asked, appalled.

'Of course not,' Mum said at once. 'Dominic, you should know better. The military are looking at it for disarming car bombs and detecting landmines and operating machinery and equipment in hazardous places, things like that. I wouldn't let them use my invention in armed combat. I'd destroy the thing first.'

'That's all right then.' I breathed a sigh of relief.

I looked from Jack to Mum and back again. Jack had a strange look on his face. A look I'd never seen before. Maybe he didn't agree with Mum that VIMS should be used for non-violent military activities only?

Mum obviously agreed with me that Jack had a strange look on his face. 'Is everything OK, dear?'

'Yes. Yes,' Jack replied immediately. 'I'm just a bit

18

worried about the demo tomorrow. I want everything to go perfectly.'

'Don't worry.' Mum laughed. 'With all the testing we've done on VIMS, it can't fail.'

'Can I go to work with you tomorrow to see the VIMS machine?' I asked hopefully.

Mum looked at me as if I'd lost my mind. 'Of course not.'

'But tomorrow's Saturday. I don't have to go to school and I promise I won't be any trouble,' I persisted. 'I'm dying to see it.'

'No.' Mum frowned.

I opened my mouth to argue some more but Mum wasn't having it.

'Dominic, which part of "no" don't you understand? Is it the "n" or the "o" that's giving you so much trouble? Jack, are you going to phone for the pizzas or shall I?'

And as far as Mum was concerned, our conversation was over.

I sat back down on the sofa, but that wasn't the end of it as far as I was concerned. I wanted to see the VIMS unit. I'd seen blueprints and schematics and I'd heard Mum and Jack talk of nothing else for the last umpteen months but I still hadn't *seen* it. What was this thing that had kept Mum and Jack so busy over the last couple of years? Maybe if I had a proper look at it instead of just seeing drawings all the time, I wouldn't mind Mum spending so much of her time with the thing. At least then, I'd know *why*. I'd know what the fascination was.

Besides, I was tired of raving on about it to my friends when I hadn't even seen it. Well, all that was going to change. A secret smile crept across my face. My mind was made up. In that moment, I decided that rain, shine, sleet or snow, tomorrow I was going to see VIMS in action.

Chapter Three

Getting In

It was yukky weather. A blustery wind blew the rain every which way so that it didn't matter which way I turned, I still got soaked. Typical late winter weather. I hate winter. It's dismal and depressing and always makes my leg hurt worse.

I glanced at Liam. He looked nervous. 'You OK?'

Liam nodded.

Who's Liam? He's my friend. A good friend. Probably my best friend actually.

'Come on then.' I opened one of the front doors of Desica International and we went inside.

'Dominic? Your mum didn't tell me she was expecting you today.'

'Hi, Mike.' I smiled wanly at the security guard behind the reception desk. For once I would've preferred it if Gareth, one of the other early morning security guards, was on the desk. He never took any notice of me, whereas Mike always chatted away. This

21

was one occasion when I didn't want to be noticed.

'So what brings you to our neck of the woods?' Mike smiled.

'Mum forgot her key card.'

'I know.' Mike sighed. 'I had to issue her with a temporary one for the day.'

'She'd forget her teeth if she didn't keep them in a glass by her bed,' I told Mike. 'She sees them as soon as she wakes up each morning and yet sometimes I still have to remind her that she's about to leave the house with only her gums on show!'

Mike stared at me. 'Your mum has false teeth?!'

I burst out laughing. 'You won't tell her I told you that, will you?'

Mike gave me a wry look, verging on disapproval. 'I should've known this was another of your wind-ups!'

'Had you going though, didn't I?' I grinned.

'Yes, you did. OK. Pass the key card here then. I'll make sure she gets it.'

'Actually, I wanted to see Mum to talk to her about something else.' As Mike's smile faded, I added quickly, 'It's very important, otherwise I wouldn't bother her. Not today of all days. I know how busy she is with the VIMS demo.'

Mike looked from me to Liam and back again. 'OK. I'll write out two passes, but once you've spoken to your mum, you're to come right back down here. D'you understand?'

'Yes, Mike. Thanks.'

I watched, holding my breath as Mike wrote us into the visitors book before writing out the passes. As he gave them to us, Mike said, 'Wish your mum luck for me.'

'I will,' I said, and grabbing Liam's arm, I made a bee-line for the lifts.

'Dominic, this is nuts!' Liam muttered. 'If we get caught . . .'

'This was your idea too, not just mine.'

'My idea! It was not!' Liam spluttered at me. 'You're the one who phoned me and said that we should try to sneak into the testing area to see your mum's new project.'

'You didn't exactly tell me to hop on my bike!' I reminded him. 'You certainly didn't say no – not until now at any rate.'

We stepped into the lift and I pressed the button for the first floor, even though Mum's office was up on the fifth floor.

'It's just that . . . I'm sure the security guard will notice if we don't give back our badges and leave soon.' Liam didn't look at all happy.

'Yes, I know. I was thinking that as well,' I admitted. 'But hopefully we can see the VIMS unit in action then sneak out of one of the emergency doors and back up to reception without anyone seeing us and before Mike sends out a search party.'

'What've I let myself in for?' Liam shook his head as

we stepped cautiously out of the lift. 'Why do I always let you talk me into these things?'

I flashed my best 'swashbuckler-on-an-adventure' smile at him and we got going. You should've seen us then! We slunk, we skulked, we tip-toed, we ducked and dived and raced down the corridor like two people in a spy film. I glared down at my leg, ordering it not to give out on me. Oh, didn't I mention? – I walk with a slight limp. I was born with one of my legs slightly shorter than the other and even though I spent months and months with my leg in plaster when I was a baby, it still didn't cure the problem. My leg is better than it has been, but it's by no means perfect. And occasionally it gives out on me altogether, although not as often now as it used to do.

But where was I? Oh yes! So there we were, skulking down the corridor, desperate not to be seen. Luckily, there were offices and partitions all over this floor and no one was taking too much notice of us. I wanted to get to the service lift but it was on the other side of the building. I reckoned this was the most dangerous part of my plan. If we got caught here, Liam and I would be out on our ears.

By the time we were both outside the service lift, my heart was charging like a rhino with the serious hump!

'We did it!' I exclaimed.

'So far so good . . .' came Liam's cautious reply.

Honestly! Sometimes he can put a real damper on things. Like two weeks ago. Listen to this. We were at the cinema watching a really funny movie – at least, I thought it was funny. And there was one bit which had me laughing so hard, I thought I'd bring back up my popcorn and hot dogs. And it wasn't just me. The whole cinema was on the floor. I glanced across at Liam and d'you know something? He was smiling. I mean, *smiling*. And only just at that! Afterwards, when I asked him about it, d'you know what he said?

'I thought it was hilarious!'

'Why didn't you laugh then?' I asked, exasperated.

'I did. I was laughing inside,' Liam told me.

'Why don't you laugh on the outside too, like most normal people?' I said.

And then he gave me one of his smiles and didn't answer. I hate it when he gives me one of his special smiles. It says, 'I know something you don't!' all over it! It drives me nuts.

'Come on then. What're you waiting for?' Liam asked impatiently.

Which stopped me daydreaming, I can tell you. I took out Mum's key card and held it up in front of the security panel. The security doors leading out to the service lift clicked open. We practically threw ourselves past the doors and I pressed the button to call the lift.

'Almost there.' I tried to sound reassuring, but my

voice was a bit shaky.

Telling myself to get a grip, I stepped into the lift to be followed by Liam. Once I pressed the button for the basement, I knew then that this was for real. I was going to see Mum's top-secret project. At last. Finally. I'd *done* it!

In the basement, I eyed the main double doors which led to the testing area. Just beyond them . . .

'I want to go,' Liam said suddenly. 'Let's go – now.'

I couldn't believe my ears. 'You're joking – right?'

Liam shook his head.

'D'you really want to leave? I mean, we're here now,' I asked carefully. 'All we have to do is go through that door and we'll see VIMS in action. You're the one who's been pestering me for a look at VIMS.'

'But I don't want us to get into trouble.'

'We won't get into trouble because Mum and the others won't be down here yet.' I glanced at my watch. 'We have a good ten minutes before anyone else appears.'

I could see that Liam was wavering. 'Come on, Liam. We'll just take a quick look at VIMS to see what all the fuss is about and then we'll come out. OK?'

'You're sure we won't get caught?'

I grinned. Liam wasn't going to bail on me! 'Don't worry. I've got it all figured out. No one will even know we were in the room.'

And I did have it all figured out. It helps when your mum is one of the people chiefly responsible for the design of the testing area. The whole of the basement of the building was given over to the testing area – and it was huge. Bigger than a football pitch. There were a number of testing labs on one side of the basement. But at least half of the basement was given over to Testing Room One. And that was where the VIMS unit was. There were a number of fire exits all around the basement, some of which led into the corridors but some of which led directly to the outside of the building. I knew we couldn't use those exits to sneak into the testing area from the road. They couldn't be opened from outside, plus they were all alarmed.

'Come on,' I urged. 'We don't have long. We'll go in, take a quick look around and then out again. The SAS would be proud of us.'

'Well, OK. If you're sure you know what you're doing,' Liam said doubtfully.

'Don't I always!' I grinned.

'No!' Liam replied at once. 'That's the trouble.'

I huffed indignantly. Liam's lack of confidence in me was totally underwhelming.

We entered the double doors. And it was like entering another world. It was more than I'd ever imagined it could be. It was vast for a start. Filing cabinets and shelves and desks and computers lined the walls. There were a number of exits all around the room and lots of fluorescent lights on the ceiling which looked like something out of an *Alien* film. I took in all these incidental, inconsequential things like someone who eats their veggies and the so-so stuff on their plate first before allowing themselves to get to the best bits. There was a medium-sized red car against the far wall. I vaguely wondered why it was there before turning to the thing I really wanted to see. In the middle of the testing area was the VIMS unit.

'Wow!' Liam breathed.

Me? I couldn't say a word. I walked slowly over to the VIMS unit, taking my time and yet longing to get there. Now I could understand why Mum was so proud of her creation. It was *stunning*. There's no other word for it. It was like something out of science fiction but it wasn't fiction, it was fact. How to describe it . . . I'll start from the bottom and work my way up! It was balanced on two metal tripods which had to be its version of feet. Attached to these, however, were wheels. I assumed that this was so that it could 'walk' on its tripod-like feet – or run on wheels. Above these, it had a number of short, jointed metal strips. We only have one joint in each of our legs – our knees – but the VIMS unit had four or five that I could see. They were all folded down, one on top of the other, with a number of cables and wires running along them. And sitting on these folded-up 'legs' was the main body of the thing. It was a cuboid in shape, rectangular and smaller than I expected. It had a monitor at the front along with a number of other buttons and circuits and lights. At each side of the box-like main body were 'arms' folded in on themselves just like its legs. At the end of each 'arm' were at least eight or nine 'fingers'. Each finger was a tool slightly different from the others and the whole lot was mounted on a revolving disc. Its fingers were like the contents of a Swiss Army knife. And at the top of the box was a smoky-grey dome-like structure which had to be its head. It had a section running around the middle of the dome which looked like an elongated black visor. It looked bizarre and exciting and wonderful all at once.

'Oh no! Quick!'

I hardly heard Liam. I carried on staring at the VIMS unit. Mum said VIMS was an artificial intelligence masterpiece and I believed her. I stood still watching it, wondering if it was switched on and watching me. Was it studying me? What did it make of me?

'Dominic, come on. I can hear them coming.' Liam grabbed my arm and pulled me towards the nearest set of filing cabinets. Only just in time too. The door opened the moment Liam and I ducked down behind the cabinets.

'You moron! What's the matter with you? D'you want us to get caught?'

'Sorry. I was totally caught up in the VIMS unit,' I whispered back.

'I thought you said we had plenty of time before your mum came down here. Now what?' Liam hissed at me.

'Now we scarper.' I had a quick look around, then pointed. 'That way, towards the exit at the back there. That'll take us into the corridor outside and then we can sneak back to the service lift.'

We crawled on our stomachs, commando-style, past boxes and crates which were good cover. But all at once the cover stopped. We had another eight or nine metres to go before we got to the next set of filing cabinets and there was absolutely nothing to hide us.

'Ladies and gentlemen, I'm sure you're all as keen as I am to get right to it. So let's start the demonstration right away,' Mum announced.

I peeked out from behind my crate. Mum stood next to Jack with Abby, her assistant, on the other side of her. There were a number of men and women wearing suits and military uniforms standing behind Mum. The others on the VIMS project stood behind them. Mum had on her 'I'm a serious scientist' face. If she caught me in here, my life wouldn't be worth living. Mum walked further into the testing area. Jack moved over to the control desk in one corner of the room.

'I have every confidence that by the end of this

demonstration, you will all see the potential of what we are trying to achieve here. The power of VIMS is only limited by our own imaginations. VIMS can do anything that we can do, only it can do it better, faster and more efficiently. For example' – Mum nodded in Jack's direction – 'VIMS can make itself flat enough to work beneath cars to disarm a car bomb.'

At her words, VIMS unfurled like a flag and then re-arranged its limbs and stretched out so that the whole thing was no higher than its main body.

'There are a number of monitoring devices built into the unit so that we can see at all times just what the VIMS unit can see.' Mum pointed to a large screen I hadn't noticed before. There on the monitor was a blue-tinted image of Mum standing with the suits and uniforms. 'VIMS also has infra-red detectors to allow it to move, see and assess any situation at night. VIMS can also grow to over three metres when the situation requires it.' Once again, Mum nodded at Jack.

Liam and I watched, amazed, as VIMS' limbs clicked and whirred and drew apart vertically like a telescope being pulled out to its maximum length. By the time the VIMS unit had finished it was at least three metres high. I mean, it was *huge*. I couldn't believe that the little squat, shoebox-like thing we'd just seen could turn into something so big and overpowering. I looked at the crowd behind Mum. One or two of them were stepping backwards surreptitiously. Mum nodded at Jack again. He pressed another button. VIMS took a heavy step forward, then another and another. Only Mum and her staff didn't move. The suits and uniforms were tripping over themselves trying to get away from the thing.

'It's perfectly OK.' Mum smiled at them. She walked over to the VIMS unit and took hold of one of its hands. It towered over her like a Goliath. Anxiety flashed through me. And then reason took over. VIMS was perfectly safe. *Mum* had designed it. I knew that she hadn't done it alone, not by any means, but in that moment, I was so proud of her. It was as if she was the first person from Earth to land on the moon. Or the first person on Earth to climb Mount Everest.

'Good morning, VIMS! How are you today?'

'I am fine, thank you.'

Liam and I weren't the only ones to gasp at that point. I had no idea the thing could talk.

'Everything functioning OK?'

'Yes, thank you,' VIMS repeated in its monotone. It sounded a bit like a woman with a deep voice trying to speak with her head in an empty bucket. VIMS folded in on itself then until it was down to its small, squat size.

'Now then,' Mum continued. 'Let's really get down to it.'

Chapter Four

The Demonstration

'We'll begin by showing everyone just what you're capable of.' Mum walked over to the control panel and picked up what looked like sunglasses and a thick dark-coloured glove. She put them on as she walked back to her audience. 'VIMS can be operated via the main control panel or by using these two virtual reality control units.' Mum tapped her glasses and held up her gloved hand. 'The glasses allow me to see what VIMS sees, almost as if I'm an actual part of the VIMS unit. And I can manipulate and manoeuvre it with this specially designed glove. Different finger movements and hand positions allow me to direct it and control it. A special microphone in my glasses also allows me voice communication over several hundred kilometres if necessary.'

'That's all very well,' piped up a woman in a dark blue uniform with a lot of ribbons and stars on her jacket. 'But what exactly do you have in mind for this . . . this contraption of yours?'

Mum smiled – which is more than I would've done if I'd been asked the same question in that sneering tone of voice.

'I haven't limited my thinking. VIMS can be used for anything you can imagine, from strong-arm work like pulverizing concrete to something as delicate as holding a baby.'

There were more than a few sceptical looks at that, but Mum continued.

'I see no reason why by this time next year, VIMS shouldn't be performing intricate surgery, undertaking rescue missions from earthquakes, underground caves, et cetera. The list is endless. That's what we've designed it to do and that's what it can do. Let me give you just a taste of what I mean. VIMS, there's a suspect car over in the corner. Maximum caution is advised.'

'Of course, Carol,' VIMS replied.

The suits and uniforms shuffled a bit closer as VIMS rolled over to the red car. It rose up on its legs until it was about one metre high, then moved around the car very carefully without touching it, as if searching for something.

'I've set up a smoke bomb in the car to simulate a car bomb. VIMS is programmed and equipped to disarm bombs . . .'

'How can a machine disarm a bomb?' a uniform asked dubiously.

'VIMS has the most sophisticated artificial intelligence of any machine in the world,' Mum told him. 'I designed it myself. Not only is it programmed with information about different types of bombs and devices, but it can also think for itself, improvise and make decisions. That's what's so unique about our machine.'

I grinned at Liam. That was my mum, that was!

'Device detected,' VIMS reported.

All attention was back on the VIMS.

'I shall attempt . . . I shall attempt . . .' And then without warning, VIMS slammed into the car.

It made me jump.

A stunned silence echoed throughout the testing room. VIMS slammed into the bonnet again. And again. And again. There was a hiss and all of a sudden smoke started billowing out from beneath the car.

All the suits and uniforms started looking at each other.

'Not much evidence of intelligence there, Dr Painter,' a suit said with sarcasm.

I wanted to rush over to him and kick him in the shins.

'I don't . . .' Mum made a fist with her gloved hand and then pulled it towards her chest. VIMS continued to slam into the car. She ran over to the control panel, where Jack was busily pressing buttons. Mum pushed

Jack to one side as she studied the monitor before her. And still VIMS kept slamming into the car. Smoke was beginning to fill the testing area now. It was horrible. It was all going wrong. The suits and uniforms started coughing. Then VIMS stopped and returned to its normal size. Seconds later it rolled off in the direction of the suits and uniforms.

'Intruder alert! Intruder alert!'

The suits and uniforms scattered to the four winds. There was yelling and screaming and smoke continued to billow out from the car.

'INTRUDER ALERT! . . . INTRUDER ALERT!'

'VIMS, what're you talking about?' I saw Mum stand in front of VIMS now. It was like looking at her through fog that was getting thicker by the second.

'Dominic, we'd better get out of here,' Liam hissed.

'Desica International staff are as previously defined. Guests are as previously defined. Two unknown intruders. Do you require further details?' VIMS asked Mum.

I sat back against the wall at once. Liam had the same idea. But we were too late. Our cover was blown.

'Where are they?' Mum asked quickly.

'Let's go,' I said quickly.

'How? We can't.' Liam's voice was frantic. 'I can't see the exits any more.'

'Over there.' I pointed in the direction of what I hoped was the nearest exit.

There was a loud whirring noise and then I heard VIMS' heavy footsteps, heading in our direction.

'Run!' Liam shouted.

And he sprang up and sprinted for the emergency door. I tried to stand but my bad leg chose that moment to give out from under me. I collapsed back down onto the floor. Pushing my hands against the floor, then the wall, I tried to stand again. Only by this time Mum was in front of me – and she was twenty shades of livid.

Chapter Five

Roasted

'Dominic, how could you?'

'Mum, if you'd just let me explain . . .'

'Explain what? How you ruined my demonstration?'

'That's not fair.'

'Not only is it fair, it's also accurate,' Mum insisted.

Liam had been sent home in disgrace after a tongue-lashing from Jack and my mum. I'd tried to tell them that it was my idea and my fault but that'd gone down like a lead balloon and Liam had still got it in the neck for following my lead. And now I was sitting in Mum's office and it was my turn. I didn't know what to do for the best. Should I bow my head and let Mum rage on at me, throwing in the occasional sorry whenever necessary, or should I try to defend myself? The mood Mum was in, one spoken word in my defence would probably have me grounded for the next millennium but at the same time, it wasn't all my fault.

'Do you realize how many months, how many years

of hard work have possibly been ruined because of your reckless behaviour?' Mum ranted. 'We needed to get more funding from those people at the demonstration and now, thanks to you, they've gone away thinking that I've spent the last years of my life working on a talking pile of junk.'

'I'm sorry.'

'What did you think you were doing?'

'I just wanted to see VIMS in action,' I muttered. Mistake.

'You had no right, Dominic. No right. This isn't a game to me. This is my living. This is my career. This is my *life* you're trying to ruin.'

'That's not fair either,' I protested. 'I'm not trying to ruin your career or your life. I'm sorry, OK?'

And I was sorry – except the words came out all flip and defensive. Because I was hurt. I know Mum didn't mean it that way, but it was as if she was saying that VIMS was her life – and I wasn't.

'No, it's not OK. It's a long way from being OK!' Mum yelled. 'The VIMS project requires more money and thanks to your selfish behaviour, we are extremely unlikely to get it.'

'It wasn't all me.' I tried to defend myself. 'VIMS started slamming into that car before it even knew that Liam and I were in the room.'

'No doubt you fiddled with the control panel

before we arrived in the testing room,' Mum sniffed.

'I didn't touch it,' I said indignantly. 'Neither did Liam.'

'So you say.' Mum didn't believe me. 'But you must've touched something you shouldn't for VIMS to behave in that way.'

'I'm telling you, we didn't touch a thing. We're not stupid. I knew you had a big demo on today. Liam and I just wanted a quick look at VIMS and then we were going to leave but you all arrived too soon.'

'So it's our fault, is it?'

'I never said that,' I sighed.

This was hard work, and the worst thing of all was, what if Mum was right? What if I had inadvertently blown her chances of getting further funding for her VIMS project. What if all those years of work were down the drain because of *me*? I'd only wanted to look at it. I hadn't wanted all this to happen.

Mum flopped down in her chair and rubbed her forehead with tired fingers. 'Dominic, you have no idea what you've done. It took many months of planning to get all those people together on one day. It took months of testing and re-testing to make sure that nothing would go wrong today and just like that you come along and . . .' Mum's lips clamped shut.

'And ruin it. You don't have to say it again. I've ruined your project and your life.'

'Don't be ridiculous.'

'I'm not being ridiculous. You said it, I didn't.'

Mum looked at me, her expression a mixture of disappointment and weariness and anger. And somehow that look was worse than all the ranting and raging. I'd let her down and we both knew it.

'I really am sorry, Mum,' I said. 'Is there anything I can do?'

'Dominic, I think you've done enough, don't you?' Mum said quietly.

At that moment, Mum's boss Julie Resnick appeared outside Mum's office. Most of the offices in Mum's building had all-glass doors and interior glass walls. Mum was always complaining about how it was like working in a fish bowl alongside a host of other fish bowls and how she couldn't even pick her nose with any degree of privacy. And all that glass meant that if the air conditioning broke down – which it often did – they all roasted.

'Carol, can I have a word, please?' Julie opened the door and spoke to Mum whilst looking directly at me.

I knew what that conversation was going to be about.

'Dominic, wait outside my office,' Mum ordered. 'And you are not to move. D'you understand?'

I nodded. Of course I understood. I was stubborn, not stupid.

The moment the office door was shut, Julie laid into Mum. I couldn't hear every word, just ninety-nine per cent of them. Julie was furious.

'I have just finished apologizing to all our guests for your son's behaviour,' said Julie. 'And believe me, your son hasn't done our project or the company any favours. A number of our visitors wanted to know what kind of amateur-hour operation we're running here!'

'I know, Julie. It was inexcusable.' Mum nodded.

'I tried to rearrange another date for the demonstration but a number of our guests made it clear in no uncertain terms that they will not be coming back.'

Mum turned to look at me, her expression stony. I swallowed hard and looked away.

'Maybe if I spoke to them?' Mum ventured.

'And said what?'

'I could tell them the truth. That it was just an unfortunate glitch and that another demonstration, any time they say, will prove that. In fact, I'm going to field test VIMS at the BFC power plant this afternoon . . .'

'No way,' Julie interrupted.

'But I already cleared this with you. And I promised Rayner,' argued Mum.

'No, Carol,' Julie insisted. 'We need to find out what went wrong this morning before exposing VIMS to anyone or anything else – and Jack agrees with me. Quite apart from that, you have a presentation and demonstration to give the board of directors on Monday morning – or had you forgotten?'

'That'll be a doddle,' Mum dismissed.

'That's what you said about the fiasco this morning!'

'Look, I think we should still go through with the field test this afternoon, just to—'

'Carol, no! I mean it. I suggest you spend the rest of the weekend finding out what went wrong with VIMS and fixing it. If the demonstration on Monday goes wrong, the project will be cancelled and then we'll all be out of a job. I don't know about you but I have a mortgage and bills to pay.'

'OK, Julie. OK.'

'I'm going to spend the rest of the day trying' – it was Julie's turn to look at me now – 'trying to repair the damage.'

And with that, Julie flung open Mum's office door and strode off. She marched straight past me without saying a word. Usually Julie smiled and asked me how I was feeling, what I was up to or doing at school and other general chit-chat. But not today. I was definitely *not* flavour of the month.

'Mum, I—'

'Go home, Dominic.'

'Mum, please. If you'll—'

'I said go straight home. I've got some thinking to do,' Mum told me harshly.

Without another word, I grabbed my bag off her office floor and headed down the corridor.

'I don't care what you and everyone else thinks,' I shouted back at her after I'd managed to swallow down what felt like a concrete block stuck in my throat. 'I didn't touch your stupid machine and neither did Liam. If it didn't work then it had nothing to do with us.'

'Go home,' Mum called out again.

And she slammed her office door shut.

Chapter Six

Sabotage

Jack and I were in the kitchen preparing Saturday's dinner – spaghetti bolognese with lamb mince. At least, that's what Jack was doing. I was slouching about getting in his way mostly. Occasionally I'd give the mince a half-hearted stir but that was about it.

'Are you still angry with your mum?' Jack asked.

The shrug of my shoulders was so slight, I'm not surprised Jack missed it.

'Well, are you?' Jack prompted.

'I'm the one who messed up her demonstration. I'm the one who made all the suits and uniforms back off, unimpressed. I could cost Mum her project, even her job. Why should I be angry?'

Jack smiled drily. 'I agree with you – your mum's the one who should be angry, not you. But that doesn't alter the fact that you are.'

'Liam and I didn't touch VIMS.' The words exploded from me.

Jack's smile vanished. He and I regarded each other.

'You believe me, don't you?' I asked uncertainly.

'Of course I believe you.'

'Do you?'

'Yes,' Jack said, his voice serious.

'Thanks,' I breathed. 'It's nice to have someone on my side for a change.'

'But that still doesn't excuse what you did.'

'I know.' I sighed. 'I've been racking my brains all day, trying to come up with a way to make it up to Mum but I can't think of anything.'

'I think your best bet is to stay out of your mum's way for a couple of hours when she gets home,' said Jack.

'What d'you suggest? Should I hide under the table? I'll tell you what! If you cut a hole in the skirting board, I'll try to disappear through it.'

'That's exactly the wrong tone to take if you want to get back in your mum's good books,' Jack told me evenly.

'Don't worry. I've got more sense than that,' I sniffed. I glanced up at the kitchen clock. 'Where is Mum anyway? It's past six o'clock.'

'I was wondering that myself,' Jack said.

An hour later, Jack and I sat down for dinner and Mum still hadn't arrived. We started eating in a strange, gloomy silence. And then I heard a key in the front door. I wanted to leap up and run into the hall, but something held me back. Mum came into the living room. I put down my fork and spoon and looked at her. And that one look told me that Mum's mood hadn't changed from that morning. No, I take that back. Her mood had changed. It was worse. She obviously hadn't had a very successful day. Jack was at her side in a moment.

'All right, love?' Jack said gently.

'No.'

'Couldn't you find out what the problem was with VIMS? Maybe if I went into work with you tomorrow . . .'

I groaned inwardly but had the sense to keep my mouth shut. I hated it when Jack and Mum worked at the weekends, especially on Sundays. I should've been used to it by now, but I wasn't.

'There's no need. I found out what the problem was. Now I just have to find a way to fix it,' said Mum.

'Isn't that good news?' Jack frowned. 'Why the long face?'

'Because I've checked and rechecked and there's only one possible explanation for what happened to VIMS today.'

'Which is?'

'He was sabotaged.'

I stared at Mum. 'What d'you mean – sabotaged?'

'Just what I said,' Mum replied grimly. 'Someone reprogrammed VIMS so that when I ordered caution on approaching the car, he interpreted the command as moving an obstruction out of the way. That's why he kept slamming into it. The car was against the wall so he didn't get very far but that's what he was trying to do.'

And even though I heard Mum say the words, I kept trying to convince myself that I'd heard her wrongly. That somehow I was misinterpreting what she was telling us.

'So who reprogrammed him?' Jack asked.

'I don't know − yet. But it was done either late last night or early this morning and reprogramming VIMS before a demonstration is strictly forbidden unless it's cleared through me first.'

'How d'you know it was reprogrammed?' I asked. 'Maybe VIMS just . . . got its wires crossed or something!'

'VIMS did not get his wires crossed,' Mum said icily.

'But Dominic does have a point,' Jack ventured. 'Maybe something happened to one of VIMS' circuits . . .'

'You two aren't listening to me,' Mum said impatiently. 'VIMS WAS SABOTAGED!'

'I can't believe it, Carol. I mean, who would do . . . ? You must've made a mistake.' Jack didn't get any further.

Mum flared up like a rocket on bonfire night. 'And I'm telling you, I haven't.'

'How can you be so sure?' Jack asked.

'Because four days ago I added a special program to VIMS' system.'

I opened my mouth, but Jack got in before me.

'What kind of special program?'

'A special diagnostic protocol.'

Mum and Jack regarded each other.

'I thought the diagnostic protocol was Mario's project and that it wasn't working yet?' Jack said.

'I took it over last month and that's what I've been spending every spare second working on for the last three weeks,' Mum informed him. 'I was determined that if, on the slim off-chance something *did* go wrong today, I'd be able to get straight to the source of the problem.'

'You didn't tell me that.' Jack shook his head.

'I can't come running to you with every work-related problem I may have. I'm meant to be the Project Manager. Besides, I didn't want to worry you.' Mum sighed. 'And I didn't want to jinx the demo. I thought it'd be almost like admitting that I was *expecting* something to go wrong.'

'What's a diag-whatsit, diagnostic protocol?' I asked. It sounded like a brand of insect spray. Or a James Bond film title!

Mum turned to me. 'It's just a special program that records who changes, adds or deletes which lines of code and it also monitors any other changes to VIMS' system. And it also allows me to step through VIMS' instructions, one line at a time or one function at a time. Luckily for me, I was able to trace through step by step and instruction by instruction just what VIMS was doing before he went haywire. It's a faster and more efficient way of checking for errors in VIMS' programming. That's why I know which part of VIMS' programming was changed.'

'And that's what you've been doing all day?' I asked.

Mum nodded. 'I was checking through to see what went wrong but then I found that a number of sections of code had been changed. It's taken me this long to check and recheck my facts.'

'So there's no doubt about it? It was sabotage?' Jack said sombrely.

Mum nodded again.

'Who did it?' I asked Mum.

Mum's expression became even more grim. 'I wish I knew. When I connected up VIMS to his control panel, all the diagnostic reports were supposed to be loaded up from him onto my computer system, but someone got in before me. All the relevant files that would've identified who did this have been deleted.'

'I thought you were the only one who was working late to look into VIMS' problems,' I said.

'By the time I realized what had happened, everyone else had gone home. But that doesn't mean that the saboteur couldn't have deleted the files before he or she left.'

'Can't you get them back?'

'Whoever deleted the files knew what they were doing. I tried to retrieve them off my computer's hard disk but the sections of the disk containing the data I wanted have been over-written with a number of large files, all full of gibberish. There was no way to get back any of the previous information on the disk.' Mum shook her head.

'D'you have any way of finding out who's responsible?' asked Jack.

'I've still got a move or two left.' For the first time since Mum had set foot through the living-room door, a faint trace of a smile flitted across her face. 'I'm hoping that the person who deleted the files at work didn't realize that VIMS routinely sends out two debug logs. One to the computer at work and one to my computer upstairs. They may have deleted the files at work but there's no way they could've got their hands on the ones here.'

'Who d'you suspect?' Jack asked. 'A rival firm?'

Mum's laugh held derision. 'Hardly! The culprit is a lot closer to home than that.'

I looked from Mum to Jack. I didn't need to look in a mirror to know that he had the same kind of shocked frown on his face as I had on mine.

'I'd have thought it was obvious,' Mum continued. 'The person who sabotaged VIMS works at Desica. The person who did it is one of my own team.'

Chapter Seven

Moves

'You can't be serious,' Jack scoffed.

But the expression on Mum's face left no room for doubt. I couldn't believe it. Sabotage! And by someone who worked with Mum every day. Someone who was on Mum's project. One of Mum's *friends*! I knew every-one on Mum's project. There was Abby, Mum's assistant, Julie, Mum's boss, Jack of course, Mario, Louis, Caryl and Jennifer, the programmers. And then the three who worked in the QA department. It took me almost a year to figure out that QA or Quality Assurance was what the VIMS software and hardware testers called them-selves. I knew all of them. I'd been to most of their houses and they'd all certainly been over to our house on numerous occasions. How could it possibly be one of them? But I know my own mum well enough to realize that she wouldn't dream of saying such a thing unless she was convinced she was right.

'So what're you going to do now?' I asked.

'I'm going to start up the computer upstairs, link up to VIMS at work and then go through the whole system with a fine-toothed comb. I'll find out who ruined my demo and when I do . . .' Mum's voice was so hard it could've cut glass.

'Have your dinner first,' said Jack gently.

'No, I . . .'

'Carol, dinner first!' Jack insisted. 'I know you. You probably haven't eaten all day and you're going to analyse the data on your computer until doomsday if you have to. So have something to eat first. The data isn't going to run off in the meantime.'

Mum didn't look too sure – about the data running off, I mean. I could see that she was bursting to argue, but when Jack's voice goes quiet but firm like that, he doesn't budge from his point of view. And trying to make him is a total waste of time. Jack doesn't put his foot down very often, but boy, when he does, it doesn't shift!

'What is it?' At Jack's puzzled look, Mum added, 'For dinner. What is it?'

'Spag bol and dolled-up ice cream!' I told her.

Jack gave me a look. 'I think we can do a bit better than that, Dominic! Madam, tonight we 'ave spaghetti bolognese, with my own special sauce,' Jack told her in a fake Italian accent that sounded more Chinese than anything else. 'Eet is topped with freshly grated

Parmesan cheese, to be followed by vanilla ice cream with raisins and an acacia honey sauce.'

Which is exactly what I said!

Mum dumped her bag on the floor and smiled. She actually looked a little less wound-up. I wouldn't go so far as to say that she was relaxed but she was a lot better than she was when she'd first entered the room. I grinned at Jack. He really was a star! I could've argued with Mum about having something to eat first until the cows came home and went to sleep and it would've got me precisely nowhere!

Mum sat down at the table, while Jack went into the kitchen to get her dinner. I reckoned it would be all dried out and horrible by now but I certainly wasn't going to say that.

'How're you feeling, Mum?' I asked.

'Tired.' Mum rubbed her eyes.

And angry and disappointed. I could read a lot more on her face than just tiredness.

'I'm sorry your demo didn't go very well today.' I floundered, searching for something to say that would make her feel better. Then it occurred to me. 'But at least now you know that it wasn't Liam and me who caused VIMS to crack up.'

The moment the last word had passed my lips, I knew I'd said entirely the wrong thing. Mum glared at me.

'I'm glad you're happy,' she sniffed.

'I didn't mean it like that. I meant . . .'

'Not now, Dominic. OK? I'm going to wash my hands.'

Mum stood up and left the room. Jack came back in carrying a plate full of steaming food.

'Where's your mum?'

'She's gone to wash her hands.'

Jack sighed. 'What did you say to her?'

Being around someone who's right all the time can be wearing, not to mention more than a little annoying. I scowled at Jack, then my scowl faded. This wasn't about me. It was about Mum and she was upset.

'All I said was that at least this proves that Liam and I had nothing to do with VIMS going out of control. I wasn't gloating. I just meant that at least Mum doesn't have to worry about Liam and me ruining her demo.' At Jack's raised eyebrow, I amended, 'Well, we didn't sabotage the VIMS unit at any rate.'

'That's true.' Jack nodded.

I was surprised. I'd expected him to blow up at me and tell me not to be so selfish. Mum soon came back into the room. Jack cuddled her, then pulled out a chair for her to sit down.

'So what's our first step after dinner?' Jack asked.

'We set up the remote link to VIMS, then analyse the debug files which will hopefully be on my system upstairs,' Mum replied before taking her first mouthful of spaghetti.

'And when you find your saboteur?' Jack asked.

'I'll call the police and have him or her arrested immediately,' Mum replied grimly. And there was no need to ask if she meant it. It was obvious that she meant every single word.

Chapter Eight

Progress

For once Mum didn't argue when I followed her and Jack into her work room, which was really a converted bedroom at the back of our house. Mum kept all the equipment she needed to work on her VIMS project in there and that's why usually I wasn't allowed in without her. In this room were two state-of-the-art computers, scanners, printers, loudspeakers, even a satellite link-up. I watched as Mum and Jack buzzed around switching on everything.

'Can I help?' I asked.

'No!' Mum replied with unflattering haste. 'We can do it.'

I leaned against the bedroom door, a resentful frown on my face.

'Dominic, you're much too old to sulk,' Mum smiled.

'I'm not sulking,' I replied indignantly.

'What would you call it then?' asked Mum.

I considered. 'It may be a pout, but it's definitely not a sulk.'

'I stand corrected.' Mum and Jack exchanged a look.

I knew they were laughing at me but I refused to rise to the bait. If I got the serious hump then so might Mum, and then she'd tell me to go downstairs while she got on with her work. I didn't want that.

'So what're you doing now?' I asked.

'I'm going to check on my computer here to see if VIMS' diagnostic report has arrived,' Mum stated.

I watched as Mum's fingers moved at lightning speed across the keyboard. Jack and I looked at each other before Jack moved to stand to one side of Mum, his hand resting on her shoulder. I moved to the other side of her.

'Well?' I asked when I couldn't bear the suspense any longer.

'It's not here.'

'What d'you mean?' Jack asked sharply. 'It never arrived or the file is corrupt or what?'

'I mean, the file never arrived. According to this log file, the last diagnostic report sent by VIMS was almost a week ago when I was testing the system back at Desica. I was counting on the diagnostic report being here.' Mum's frown was razor sharp. 'I don't understand why it would work last week and not work today.'

'So what happens now?' I asked.

Mum pulled at her earlobe the way she always did when she was thinking.

'I'll have to contact VIMS and hope that it can provide some answers.'

'You're going to interrogate it?' asked Jack.

'Why not?' Mum said defensively. 'He's an artificial intelligence system. Even if the diagnostic reports have been erased, he may still know who changed the software. He should still have the necessary data in his memory.'

'It's a long shot,' Jack said sceptically.

'It's the only shot I have left,' Mum pointed out.

I watched as Mum put on the VIMS VR, or virtual reality, glove. It was black, with a number of buttons on both the front and the back of it.

'VIMS, access clearance Alpha–November 9829302–Tango Tango!' said Mum.

The big flat screen Mum had against one wall flickered into life.

'Where is VIMS?' I asked eagerly.

'You can't see him with this unit. You just see what he sees. I'd better put him in simulation mode so none of his programming is permanently changed,' Mum added, more to herself than anyone else.

'How does VIMS know when she's talking to it and when she's not?' I whispered to Jack.

'If you're in the same room, you look at him directly

to give him a command. If you're doing it remotely like this, then you just use his name before the command, so you say, "VIMS, do this!" or "VIMS, do that!" Then the unit knows you're giving him a direct command,' Jack explained.

'Why do you and Mum keep calling VIMS "him"?'

'Why do you keep calling VIMS "it"?' Jack countered.

'Because it's not real,' I replied.

'It is to me and your mother,' said Jack.

I turned back to the monitor.

'VIMS, access your memory files from yesterday morning, 0900 hours onwards,' said Mum.

'Accessing,' VIMS replied, its strange voice humming out over Mum's computer loudspeakers.

'VIMS, report any amendments, additions or deletions to your programming,' Mum ordered.

'There have been no amendments, additions or deletions in the requested time frame,' VIMS informed us.

'VIMS, when was the last time any of your programming was altered – in any way?'

'Five days, fourteen hours, seven minutes . . .'

'VIMS, OK. That's fine, thank you.'

I looked at Mum. Was it my imagination or was she more polite to VIMS than she ever was to me?!

Mum started pulling on her earlobe so hard, I

thought she was trying to get it to rest permanently on her shoulder.

'VIMS, which functions were last changed?'

'City mapping, location analysis.'

'Jack, did you authorize those changes?' Mum frowned up at him.

'No. This is all news to me,' Jack replied.

'Well, I didn't authorize them either.' Mum's frown deepened. 'But those functions have nothing to do with what went wrong with VIMS today. VIMS, who was responsible for altering those functions?'

'You,' came the immediate reply. 'New and amended code was downloaded by Carol Painter.'

'Oh, no, it wasn't.'

'Does that help?' I asked.

'No. It only confirms that the saboteur works for me. It narrows the list down a bit though. It couldn't have been any of the QA staff because they don't have access to any of my development software. And apart from Jack, Julie and me, the only other ones who would know how to change those VIMS functions are Jennifer and Mario. VIMS, simulation mode.'

Jennifer or Mario . . . Which one of them was the saboteur? To be honest it was hard to believe that either of them was.

'VIMS, low mode, silent running. VIMS, leave the Desica building, make your way to my house and then return to the Desica building – maximum caution.'

'You're bringing him here?' I couldn't believe my ears.

Moments later, VIMS made his way towards the doors. Mum mimed opening the door with her gloved hand and VIMS did it for real as I watched the monitor.

'Can VIMS really come all the way to our house and then go all the way back to Desica?' I asked, astounded.

Mum smiled. 'We've never actually tested him wheeling through the streets of our town.'

'But . . . but it's wheeling past the security guard now.' I pointed at the monitor.

VIMS was making his way to the front doors.

'VIMS, activate Desica main doors and exit and suspend security guard.'

'What did you say? Is VIMS going to hurt the guard?'

'Dominic, of course not. What you're seeing is not real. It's just a simulation.' Jack smiled.

'I don't understand.'

'We hired some professional film makers who spent weeks filming everything within a five-mile radius so that we could test VIMS' responses to various situations, night and day, crowds and no people on the street, good and bad weather conditions. Of course, all this happened before I joined the project but the film is regularly updated. We've given VIMS enough knowledge of this town so that he can create various scenarios and play them back, like playing back a DVD.'

I stared at the screen, unable to believe my eyes. 'So none of this is real? It looks exactly like VIMS has opened the Desica main doors and is wheeling out onto the pavement.'

'Yes, it does, but I'm afraid it's not real. It's all a simulation, an illusion. VIMS is playing back the data as if he is really moving through his environment, but I can assure you, he's still in the testing area in the basement of Desica, even though it looks as if he's on the main road now.'

'So why're you running this simulation, Mum?'

'VI— I mean, the unit reported that his city mapping and location analysis functions had been altered. I'm just running a quick test to see if he can make it from A to B and back again without anything going wrong.'

I stood and watched in silence as VIMS seemed to wheel through the town on his way to our house. The sky was dark and clear, with a number of people hurrying home, fighting against a chill winter wind. It all seemed so real – it was uncanny. Mum continued to direct VIMS' movements with her gloved hand and to give VIMS verbal commands which it immediately followed as if it really was on the outside.

When it reached our house, the light in Mum's bedroom at the front of the house appeared to be on. I knew it wasn't. And that's the only way I knew what

64

I was seeing wasn't real. Mum directed VIMS back to Desica, making him avoid all passers-by by using any available cover to skulk out of sight until the danger was passed.

'This is part of his training too,' Mum explained. 'There may be occasions when stealth is called for and I want VIMS to learn to judge a situation for himself.'

Finally, VIMS was back at Desica and in its training area again.

'It seems all right on the surface but I'll have to go into work tomorrow and run some proper tests. I have to give a demonstration to the board with the VIMS unit on Monday. They want to see where all their money has gone and I don't want a single thing to go wrong.'

'But Mum, I thought we were all going to the pictures tomorrow,' I protested.

'I'm sorry, but I can't go – this is urgent. I have to make sure that the demo on Monday goes without a hitch. Why don't you go to the pictures with Jack?'

'I wanted all of us to go together.'

'Well, I can't.'

I struggled to keep the disappointed scowl off my face – and failed miserably.

'But what're you going to do? Are you going to sit on VIMS until Monday morning to make sure that no one attempts to sabotage it again?' I asked.

'I don't need to,' Mum replied. 'I've changed all the access codes. No one except me can change a single line of code until after Monday's demo.'

'But, Carol—'

'No, Jack. I'm not taking any chances,' Mum interrupted. 'No one is going to touch that machine in any manner, shape or form until after the board meeting.'

'At least let me help you . . .'

'No, this is my problem. I have to sort it out myself,' Mum replied.

I only half listened as Jack and Mum argued about it. All I could think of was yet another promised trip out going up in a puff of smoke. Bitterly, I wished I was made of metal and ran about on wheels – then maybe Mum would take a bit more notice of me. Then everyone would take more notice of me and no one could push me around and even if they did, it wouldn't hurt me inside the way it always did.

Chapter Nine

Ex-Best Friend

After everything that had happened over the weekend, having to go to school on Monday was a big non-event. Liam knocked for me.

'You took your time. I was just about to leave without you. Wait a sec!' I grabbed my coat off the banister.

'Hello to you too!' Liam said.

After smiling my apology, we set off. Liam and I discussed everything that had happened over the week-end as we walked to school.

'I'm sorry I got you into trouble,' I told him.

'That's OK,' he shrugged. Then he surprised me by adding, 'Seeing VIMS at long last was worth it actually. Besides, my consolation was knowing that no matter how much trouble I was in, you were in more!'

'Thanks!'

'What are friends for?' Liam grinned.

We were just getting to the part where VIMS had

discovered us as the intruders in the testing room when we reached the school gates.

'You should've seen your face when VIMS started coming towards us,' I teased.

'My face! What about your own?' Liam said indignantly.

'How would you know what my expression was?' I scoffed. 'The moment VIMS came towards us, you leaped up and took off like a cheetah in a panic!'

'The cheetah who leaps and runs away, lives to . . .' Liam's voice trailed off.

I had just a moment to wonder at it before I was knocked to the ground from behind.

'What's the matter, Gimpy? Can't stand on your own two feet?'

I didn't need to look up to see who had pushed me. Matthew Viner. I called him Matt Vinyl behind his back. Of course, it was behind his back. I don't have a death wish. Matt Viner. What should I tell you about him first? He can't look at me without making some nasty comment about my leg or some other part of my body. What else should I tell you about him? He's about my height but there's more to him. He's chunky, in a muscle-chunky way. He has lots of friends. Oh yes, and he hates me – everyone knows that. Nobody – includ-ing me – knows why, but it's the truth. He can't stand me. What else? Not much really, except that about a year ago he used to be my best friend and he'd been my best friend since infant school.

'Come on, Gimpy. Stand up then. Or do you like grovelling on the floor?'

'Leave him alone, Matt,' Liam said quietly.

'Stay out of this,' Matt flashed back. 'This has nothing to do with you.'

'You're a real hero, aren't you?' Liam told him scornfully.

I struggled to get to my feet. My leg was suddenly aching – the way it always did whenever Matt started in on me. I looked round. Liam was glaring at Matt. Matt knew it and he didn't care. He wore the same contemptuous smile that he always did when he looked at me. The sort of smile you might wear if an ant or a fly challenged you to a punching contest. I looked at Liam again, wishing as I always did that he would back off and leave me to fight – and lose – my own battles. Matt came towards me. I knew he was going to push me over again.

'Go on then, Einstein,' I said bitterly. 'Show everyone how clever you are 'cause you can knock me to the ground. Show everyone how you've only got two brain cells – one in each bicep. Ooff!'

The pavement was my chair again and my shoulder was throbbing from where Matt had just thumped me. I struggled to my feet. Liam tried to help me up but I angrily shrugged him off.

Matt's fists were clenched. Then I saw his fingers straighten out as he relaxed. He gave me a bitingly scornful look. 'I'm not going to hit you again. I've changed my mind.'

'Let's hope your new mind works better than the old one – you pathetic little weasel,' I hissed.

It took him a couple of seconds to get it. But get it he did. And then so did I. Matt thumped my other shoulder. I scrambled up again as best I could.

Stay down, you moron, a voice inside me protested. But I ignored it – the way I always ignored my own good advice. I was going to show Matt that I wasn't afraid of him. Actually, I was scared of him and we both knew it but that didn't mean I was going to let him get the better of me. Matt drew back his fist and I knew he was going to punch my face. I tried to step back and my bad leg let me down by choosing then of all moments to stop working. I went down like a skittle – without Matt having to even touch me.

'And stay there,' Matt said scornfully. 'It's where you belong.'

'Come on, Matt,' Robert, his friend, said. 'Dominic is a total waste of time and space. I don't know why you even bother with him.'

'Neither do I.' That familiar contemptuous smile was back on Matt's face.

I wanted to kick his ankles or at least outstare

him, but as always I was the first one to look away.

His point made, Matt swaggered off with his friends.

'Are you OK?' Liam asked me. He put out a hand to help steady me. I knocked it away.

'Yes, I'm fine. Stop fussing,' I snapped.

Of course I wasn't OK. It wasn't bad enough that this had to happen, but it had to happen in front of him. I couldn't have been any more humiliated.

'I'll see you later,' I told him and I walked off, aware that my limp was even more pronounced now. I didn't have to look behind me to know that Liam was watching me go.

I couldn't concentrate for the rest of the day and more than one teacher told me off about it. I kept thinking about Matt, and trying, yet again, to figure out why he'd gone off me. I know I'm not the most riveting person in the world. I'm not stupid, but I'm not an egg-head genius either. And any sport that involves running usually doesn't involve me. I can run, but when I do I reckon I look like a camel in a panic so I don't tend to do it. I guess what I'm trying to say is that I'm just an average boy who's maybe a bit more sarcastic than average, but that's just my way. So why had Matt stopped being my friend? As I remember it, one day we were best mates and the next day we weren't. No explanations, no accusations, no nothing. Matt started going around with Robert and Ace and that lot and it took me half a term to find a new best friend – Liam. Liam and I drifted together, mainly because we had no one else to talk to. Liam takes himself very seriously, just like Mum. Funny, but when I think about it, deep down I take myself more seriously than either of them. I hadn't really thought of that before.

I spent all day trying not to think about Matt because every time I did, I could feel my face set into a plaster-of-Paris scowl. If only there was some way I could get back at him. Some way to show him that he couldn't push me around because I'd push back. Some way of . . . And then I had it! A way to get my own back without getting duffed up! It wouldn't be perfect, but it'd definitely do!

'Liam, can you come back to my house after school this afternoon?' I whispered.

'You're meant to come round to my house for tea – remember?' Liam reminded me.

'But this is important . . .'

'No, Dominic, you're coming round for tea. You've already put it off three times at the last minute. Mum's bought cakes and all sorts and I'm not showing up without you again.'

'But, Liam . . .'

'Whatever it is, it can wait until after you've had tea at my house,' Liam insisted.

'Er, d'you two mind?' Mr Brent drawled from the front of the class.

Liam and I instantly shut up. I was burning to go straight home to carry out my idea, but if I did probably neither Liam nor his mum would ever speak to me again. And whilst I didn't mind about Mrs Greene, I didn't want to lose Liam as a friend.

'OK! OK! I'll be there,' I sighed.

'What's so all-fired urgent anyway?' Liam asked, keeping a wary eye on Mr Brent.

'I've had an idea,' I grinned.

Liam regarded me, a dawning look of suspicion and alarm on his face.

'Oh no! Please, Dominic! Not another of your ideas which is going to get us into all kinds of trouble.'

'This one won't. Trust me!'

'That's usually my first mistake,' Liam sighed.

'Don't worry. You'll love it.'

'What is it?'

'You'll see.'

'Oh dear!'

I had to bite my lip to stop myself from laughing at Liam's tone. Today was going to be a great day after all. I was finally going to get my own back on Matt.

Chapter Ten

Revenge

Tea at Liam's house dragged on like an ant carrying a heavy suitcase. Liam's mum was driving me bonkers – as always.

'And how is your leg, Dom?'

Did I mention that I *hate* it when people call me Dom?

'Fine.'

'Does it give you much trouble?'

'No.'

'You were born with a defective leg, weren't you?'

'Yes.'

'How long were you in hospital for while they tried to fix it?'

'Ages.'

'You poor thing.'

'I'm fine, Mrs Greene, really I am.'

'So brave! You poor thing!'

That was usually my cue to laser Liam with my

'please-do-something-about-your-mother!' look. Liam had the good grace to look embarrassed but he still let his mum witter on about my leg. I wouldn't mind, but every time I saw her we always had the same old, tired conversation. Is it any wonder I kept bowing out of tea at Liam's house?

The moment I thought it wouldn't be rude to scarper, I was out of there! It was dark and cold as Liam and I walked to my house but it was preferable to listening to Mrs Greene spout on, it really was. Besides, all I had in my head was what I was about to do.

'So what's your brilliant idea?' Liam asked. 'Are you ready to tell me yet?'

'How d'you fancy a trek to Matt's house?' I grinned.

'Have you lost your marbles?' Liam asked seriously. 'Why on earth would you want to go round there?'

'I'm not going round there,' I replied.

Liam's eyes narrowed. 'You must be off your trolley if you think I'm going round there when you're not!'

'No, you're not going either.'

'But you just said . . .'

'Come on! I'll show you.'

From the expression on his face, I knew I'd intrigued him. I led the way to my house.

'We're going to visit Matt Viner's house without leaving my back bedroom,' I told Liam.

'You've lost me.' Liam shook his head.

'Follow me.' Opening the front door, I led the way into the house. In the hall, a light beside one of the buttons on our phone was flashing. I glanced down at the display. Seven messages! No way was I going to listen to all of those now. I'd be taking notes for Mum until next Christmas! We went upstairs and into the back bedroom where Mum kept all of her computer equipment.

'I thought you weren't allowed in here,' Liam frowned.

'Mum and Jack are working late. And as Mum says, what the eye doesn't see, the heart can't grieve about!'

'You're a real glutton for punishment,' Liam told me. 'Suppose your mum finds out?'

'She won't,' I insisted. 'But now for the good stuff. It's get-my-own-back time!'

Liam didn't say a word as we entered the room. He whistled appreciatively but that's all. I'd never taken him into Mum's work room before. Strictly speaking, it wasn't allowed. In fact, Mum would do her nut if she knew I was in her special room! I'm only allowed in it when she's already in there and usually not even then. But she wasn't here and I'd make sure nothing happened to her equipment.

I whipped around the room, switching on the computer, the monitor, the remote link and the virtual reality system.

'Dominic, what're you up to?' Liam asked, worried.

'Watch,' I told him.

It took three attempts to link up to the VIMS unit at Desica International. I'd seen Mum do it plenty of times but this was the first time I'd done it myself. Once the link had been established, I put my right hand in the VR, or virtual reality, glove. It was warm and slightly scratchy. I assumed that was because of all the sensors on the inside of the glove. I made a fist, then flexed my fingers. The monitor screen blinked on. We could see the VIMS testing area. I considered putting on the VR glasses but then Liam wouldn't have been able to see on the monitor what I was doing. And I wanted him to see every single thing. He'd been there when Matt had shown me up so it was only right that he should see I wasn't a complete wimp – that I could fight back.

'Now what?' Liam asked.

'Now we're going to have some fun,' I grinned. 'Watch! And learn! I'm going to take VIMS for a walk. Here we go!'

After a sudden lurch, it seemed as if the whole room was moving towards us. I pointed my index finger forward in the direction of the testing area double doors. VIMS started moving forward.

'What's going on?' Liam gasped.

'I'm making VIMS move forward. I'm going to make him leave the Desica building and make his way to Matt's house.'

'No!' Liam stared. 'That's really VIMS moving?'

'That's right.'

'How come we can't see him?'

''Cause we're seeing *through* him. We're seeing everything he sees, looking through his eyes if you like,' I explained.

'You can't take him out of Desica,' Liam said, appalled. 'You can't just have him trundle down the street to Matt's house.'

'Oh, yes, I can,' I laughed.

'Dominic, see sense,' Liam urged. 'Someone's bound to see him and then they'll freak out and call the police and all sorts. And when your mum hears about it . . .'

'Mum and Jack are probably up on the fifth floor in the computer room,' I said.

'Probably? I don't like the sound of that.' Liam shook his head.

I know I should've told him that VIMS was only in simulation mode. That everything he was seeing wasn't really real. It was just an illusion, like a film being played back through the VIMS unit – but I didn't want to tell him that. Not yet.

'Don't worry. I'll have VIMS back in the testing area before anyone realizes it's missing,' I said.

I pointed my index finger forward again. VIMS' surroundings appeared to move backwards, creating the illusion that VIMS was moving forwards. When it got to the door, I mimed turning the door handle. I watched on the monitor as the testing door opened. I pointed forward. The surroundings scrolled until VIMS reached the lift. I pointed at the control panel of the lift and said, 'VIMS, press the button.'

VIMS did as it was told. The lift doors opened almost immediately. I pointed into the lift and VIMS entered it. I made VIMS press the button to go up to the ground floor. When the lift doors opened, I could see on the monitor a security guard I did not recognize. He was sitting at his desk in the reception area, reading his newspaper. It took me a moment to remember the appropriate command for what I wanted to do next. Keeping my hand level and parallel to the ground, I said, 'VIMS, low mode, maximum stealth, silent running.'

Almost immediately, the monitor view changed so that we could only see a few centimetres off the ground. VIMS wheeled right past the security guard's desk to the exit.

'How're you going to open the door?' Liam asked.

'Like this! VIMS, activate Desica main doors and exit. On exit, immediately seek cover and get out of sight.'

Before our eyes, one of the main exit doors opened and VIMS rolled out.

'VIMS, rear view please.'

On the monitor we saw the security guard look up from his newspaper, surprise on his face. Mum must've updated the tape VIMS was currently playing back. That explained why I didn't recognize this particular guard, but then I couldn't know every single person who worked at Desica. With a deep frown, the guard stood up, looking at the exit door which was now swinging shut.

'VIMS, normal view – and get out of sight. Now!' I ordered.

I lost sight of the guard as VIMS rolled towards the bushes fringing the entrance to the building – but not for long. VIMS had only just managed to hide when the guard appeared at the door, looking severely puzzled and more than a little nervous. Through the sparse winter shrubbery in front of VIMS I saw the guard look out and around but there was no one to see and nothing to look at. My heart stopped when the guard looked in VIMS' direction. I was so afraid he'd seen VIMS but the guard turned his head for another look around. Then he went back inside the Desica building. I wasn't the only one who breathed a huge sigh of relief.

'Are you sure he didn't see VIMS?' Liam asked.

'I don't think so. He would've come out or raised the alarm if he had seen him,' I replied.

And only then did I remember the truth. VIMS was in simulation mode. This wasn't real. It was astounding how every little detail looked so believable, right down to the expressions on the security guard's face. He looked so amazing, so lifelike, that I'd forgotten I was just watching a simulation. No wonder Liam was so completely fooled. But I wasn't going to tell him the truth – at least, not yet. I was going to have some fun first.

I pointed my finger forward and VIMS set off again. Whenever anyone approached VIMS, I made it hide out of sight. That was mainly for Liam's benefit but I reckoned that even if it was just a simulation and all I was seeing were images being played back like playing a DVD on the TV, I should still make VIMS treat the whole thing like it was a serious exercise. I didn't want to interfere with the way it'd already been programmed or anything.

'Hang on . . . Why're you turning into Ellisnore Road?' Liam asked when ten minutes later we were finally reaching VIMS' final destination.

I grinned at him. 'I told you. We're visiting Matt Vinyl. He lives in this road. At number forty-five.'

Liam suddenly became very still. 'Dominic, what're you going to do?'

Chuckling gleefully, I turned back to the monitor. I pointed forward until VIMS reached Matt's house. I indicated that VIMS should go past the open gate and into the front garden, which was hidden from the rest of the street by a tall, untidy hedge. I made VIMS look around. Stupidly, I hadn't made VIMS take anything with it so we were going to have to improvise. There were a number of plant pots lined up behind the hedge, and in the corner of the garden, a large wheelie dustbin sat self-consciously.

'VIMS, pick up that dustbin and empty it on the ground,' I said.

'Dominic – no! You can't do that,' Liam protested at once.

'Oh no? Watch this then.'

We all watched the monitor as VIMS lifted the huge wheelie bin and flipped it over as if it were a jar of coffee. Boxes, tins, papers, old flowers – they all came tumbling out.

'Dominic, that's enough,' Liam told me sternly.

'Oh no, it isn't,' I argued. 'VIMS, pick up one of the potted plants and throw it through the window in front of you, then head back to the testing room at Desica with all possible speed.'

And that's just what VIMS did. It picked up the nearest potted plant and hurled it through the downstairs window. Then it wheeled out of the front garden moving like a bat out of hell.

I turned triumphantly to Liam. 'Ta-da!'

He wasn't smiling. In fact, he was looking at me like he'd never seen me before.

'Not even Matt would stoop so low as to pull a stunt like that,' he said.

'Of course he would – and worse.'

'I'm going home now.'

I creased up laughing. 'You should see the look on your face!' I was laughing so much, I started to sneeze. 'Don't worry. It's not real. None of it was real.'

'What're you talking about?'

'It's just a simulation. A film crew spent months filming all around this town for Mum and the VIMS project. Mum's team wanted to test VIMS' responses to various different situations without really exposing him to the world outside.'

'But we just saw VIMS go into Matt's garden,' Liam protested. 'I saw him empty the bin and throw the potted plant through the window.'

'It wasn't real. VIMS uses the stock footage of the town and then reprograms the images based on what you ask him to do.'

Liam still looked sceptical.

'I'm telling you that none of it was real,' I said, exasperated. 'That's why it's called *virtual* reality, not actual reality. I'm not too sure how all the ins and outs of it work, but believe me, when VIMS is in simulation mode he can do anything without moving outside the testing area at Mum's work place. Besides, is it likely that I'd really do that to Matt's house? Would I really get VIMS to throw things through the window? Someone could get hurt.'

Liam scrutinized me. He was trying to decide whether or not I was on another of my wind-ups! But not this time. This time I was totally serious. I think it was my last argument that finally won Liam over. His expression cleared and he turned back to the screen.

'Can VIMS really do all that – in a simulation?' Liam whistled.

I nodded.

'So it wasn't real?'

'None of it. Although I must admit, part of me would like to see Matt get what's coming to him,' I couldn't help adding.

'It's quite good,' Liam stated.

Which, coming from him, was high praise indeed.

'Honestly! As if I'd do a thing like that.' My smile faded.

In fact, the more I thought about what he'd just believed, the more annoyed I got. When I came to think about it, it wasn't very flattering. Did Liam really believe that I'd do something so destructive, so *vindictive*? Matt had provoked me enough but I wasn't about to retaliate like that.

'I think you should pack the whole thing up now, before your mum comes home or we get caught, or break something,' Liam said at last. 'It's very good, but let's call it a day.'

'OK.' I shut down the system and pulled off the VR

glove. 'You must admit though, it *was* fun. I mean, imagining that it was all for real – it was fun.'

Liam gave a slow smile. 'I guess so.'

'As they say, revenge is sweet but revenge with VIMS' help is pure strawberries and ice cream!'

The phone rang.

Liam left the room first, with me bringing up the rear. I think to be honest that Liam was glad to leave the room. It was a lot to take in all at once. He kept glancing back over his shoulder as if he still couldn't *quite* believe that what he'd just seen wasn't in the slightest bit real. When we got downstairs, I picked up the phone.

'Dominic, is that you?'

'Hi, Pops.' I grinned at the phone in my hand. Strange how just hearing my granddad's voice always made me smile. 'How're you? When are we going to see you next?'

'Where have you been? Jack and I have been phoning all afternoon.' There was no answering smile in Granddad's voice. In fact it was just the opposite.

My heart lurched in my chest. Something was wrong. 'What's the matter, Pops?'

'It's your mum,' Pops replied grimly. 'There's been an accident.'

Chapter Eleven

Out of Control

Liam insisted on staying with me until Pops came to pick me up and take me to the hospital. I sat on the second-to-last stair, staring at the front door and willing Pops to arrive.

'You don't have to do this. I'm OK,' I told Liam, more than once.

'I know that,' he replied. 'But I want to do it. Didn't your granddad give you any clue about what happened to your mum?'

'I've already told you everything he said,' I snapped. 'Mum was giving a demo of VIMS this morning and there was an accident and she was knocked unconscious.'

'But what kind of accident?'

I opened my mouth to rant at him, only to snap it shut a moment later without saying a word. He was just concerned about Mum and it would be really out of order to take out my anxiety on him.

'Liam,' I began when I could trust myself to speak without biting his head clean off, 'I've played you the phone messages Jack and Pops left on the answering machine and I've told you what Pops said to me over the phone. You know as much as I do now.'

Liam nodded slowly. 'I know, it's just that . . .'

He didn't say any more. Nor did he have to. I knew what he meant. Jack and Pops had both been deliberately unspecific when they phoned. Jack had only said that Mum was in hospital and I was to phone him on his mobile the moment I got his messages. Pops had said pretty much the same thing – except to add at the end of each of his messages how much he hated talking to bloomin' answering machines!

After what seemed like years, the door bell finally rang. I flew up and flung the door open. I gave a start of surprise. It wasn't Pops. It was Julie Resnick, Mum's boss. I stood blinking at her like a stunned owl.

'Hello, Dominic. Can I come in?'

'D'you know what's happened to Mum?' I asked.

'Can I come in?' Julie repeated.

'Yes, of course.' I stepped aside, allowing her to enter the hall.

'So what happened?' I said impatiently.

'D'you want to sit down?' Julie asked me.

No, I didn't want to sit down, or dance around, or stand on my head. I just wished she'd get on with it.

'I want you to prepare yourself,' Julie said grimly. 'Your mum's invention, the VIMS unit, went haywire again, only this time it knocked your mum off the stage she was on.'

'The stage?'

'The demonstration to the board of directors was taking place in a conference hall with a small stage. Your mum wanted to demonstrate VIMS' capabilities and to show the board a film of what she and her team have been up to over the last year.'

'And VIMS knocked her off the stage?' I couldn't take it all in.

'It went haywire and started lashing out in all directions. Your mum moved in to stop it and it hit her across the chest, knocking her off the stage,' Julie told me straight.

The door bell rang again. I opened it. This time it was Pops.

'I'm sorry it took me so long to get here,' Pops apologized at once. 'The traffic was a nightmare. Come on, let's go to the hospital.'

'Is Jack still with her?' I asked.

'As far as I know,' Pops replied.

Liam trooped out of the house ahead of us.

'Dominic, phone me first thing tomorrow and let me know how your mum is doing, OK?' Liam said.

I nodded.

I grabbed my coat and was about to make my way out the door after Liam when I realized that Julie was still in the house.

'Can I help you?' Pops asked politely.

'I'm Julie Resnick, Carol's boss,' Julie explained to Pops.

'Ah yes. You phoned me earlier,' Pops nodded.

'That's right. I hope you don't mind but I just came to make sure that Dominic was all right.'

'He's fine.' Pops frowned. 'We're both going to the hospital now.'

'Oh . . . er . . . I thought I might check through some of your daughter's programs and documents on VIMS whilst I was here . . .' said Julie.

Pops' look of astonishment rapidly turned to icy anger. He drew himself up to his full height and looked Julie straight in the eye.

'My daughter is in hospital and she's injured, not dead. There's no need to collect up all her belongings quite yet.'

'Oh, I didn't mean to . . . Of course not,' Julie stammered in her effort to placate Pops. 'I'll go. This is the wrong time to . . . I'll go.'

'I'd appreciate it,' Pops told her, frost dripping from every word.

Julie glanced behind her and up our stairs, before she sidled past Pops to leave the house.

Liam stepped aside on the garden path to let her get past. No one spoke until Julie was in her car and driving away. I took a glance at Pops then. A muscle in his cheek just under his eye was doing the samba. I'd only ever seen that particular muscle dance like that once before – when, ages ago, Pops took me to the park and some other boys had made fun of my limp.

'Let's go,' Pops said gruffly.

'Let me know how she is – OK?' Liam said.

I nodded, not trusting myself to speak.

All the way to the hospital, neither Pops nor I spoke. Pops doesn't like to talk and drive at the same time and I wasn't in the mood to speak anyway. It took ages to get to the hospital. Pops drives at least ten miles below the speed limit. He calls it 'safe driving', but judging by the dirty looks we kept getting I don't think the drivers around us would've agreed.

At last we reached the hospital. After a lot of wandering about, trying to find out where Mum was, we at last reached her ward. Mum was in a side room and we'd barely been told the number before I was running towards it and flinging open the door. And I got the shock of my life. Mum's head was swathed in bandages and she was linked up to a monitor beside her bed. And yet with all this stuff around her, Mum's eyes were closed, as if she was sleeping. That's the part that really scared me. She looked so peaceful, as if she was above and beyond everything going on around her. I stood in the doorway, watching her. My throat started to hurt and I had to swallow quite a few times before it stopped.

'Dominic, are you going to hover in the hall all night?' Pops said irritably.

Slowly I walked into the room, followed by Pops. Only when I was fully in the room did I see Jack. He was sitting slumped on a chair in the corner of the room. And his eyes were puffy and red.

'Is Mum going to be all right?' I whispered.

Jack shrugged. 'The doctors don't know yet. Apparently the next few hours are going to be crucial.'

'What exactly is the matter with her?'

'Concussion, severe bruising and a broken rib. The rib punctured her right lung but that's OK now.'

I blinked stupidly at the catalogue of injuries VIMS had inflicted on my mum. 'Where is VIMS now?'

'Back in the testing area at Desica,' Jack said.

'I hope that dangerous bag of bolts is going to be dismantled,' Pops said furiously, 'before it can harm anyone else.'

'We're still discussing that,' Jack said sombrely.

'But you can't do that. Mum would hate it.' The words exploded from me before I even realized what I was going to say. I, of all people, should've been happy about the prospect of VIMS being dismantled, but instead I was horrified. VIMS was Mum's life work. VIMS was Mum's *dream*.

'I'm sorry your mum ever started working on VIMS,' Jack said bitterly. 'I'm sorry I ever heard of the thing. I'm sorry . . . I'm sorry . . .'

And this is going to sound really mushy, I know, but that's when I realized just how much Jack loved my mum.

'It's not your fault, son,' Pops said gruffly. 'According to what that Resnick woman told me earlier, the VIMS machine just went out of control and Carol was in the wrong place at the wrong time.'

'Yes, but I should've persuaded Julie and Carol to postpone the demonstration this morning until we'd figured out what was wrong with VIMS. I did try but . . .'

'But knowing my daughter, you didn't get very far.' Pops sighed.

'I should've tried harder,' Jack said angrily.

Pops and I looked at each other. We knew Jack was angry with himself, not with us and not with Mum. Jack turned to look at me. It was the first time he'd looked away from Mum since I'd entered the room.

'Dominic, you can stay for a while and then I'm taking you back home.'

'Oh, but—'

'No, buts!' Jack interrupted. 'You've got school tomorrow.'

'But, Mum—'

'Your granddad or I will be here. We'll make sure that your mum is never alone,' Jack insisted. 'I'll pick you up after school tomorrow and bring you here so you can stay a bit longer.'

I gave up at that. Jack had that 'I've-made-up-my-mind!' look on his face.

'Do you really think VIMS will be scrapped?' I couldn't help asking.

Jack considered, then nodded slowly. 'What happened on Saturday was bad enough, but after what happened to your mum this morning . . .'

'I see.' And I did see. As Pops and I each settled into the chairs on either side of Mum's bed, my mind was working furiously. They couldn't junk Mum's project. They just couldn't. I wouldn't let that happen. But what could I do? I had to think of something – and fast. Or the past few years of Mum's life would all have been for nothing.

Chapter Twelve

A Trip to the Seaside

All the way home, I tried to think of a way to stop Desica ditching Mum's project, but it seemed like the harder I tried to come up with an idea, the bigger the headache I was getting – and that's all.

'Your mum will be fine, Dominic,' Jack said gently. 'I know she will.'

I nodded, but said nothing.

When we got home, Jack insisted that I should have a proper dinner and so we went to the kitchen and started making baked, un-battered fish and fat-free chips. Then Jack set about making a salad. If I hadn't had other things on my mind, I might've complained about all the tastiest bits being left out of the meal! But as it was, VIMS took up every corner, nook and cranny of each thought that wasn't wrapped around Mum. If only she wasn't unconscious. Even from a hospital bed, I was sure that Mum could've persuaded Julie and everyone else to leave VIMS alone – at least until she was back on her feet again. But Mum couldn't argue her case. So I had to buy her some time until she could. But how? *How?*

I picked at my meal whilst Jack sat with a piece of fish poised on his fork for over five minutes as he stared into space.

'Jack, are you all right?'

He didn't answer. I don't think he even heard me.

'Jack . . . ?'

'Sorry. Yes? What?'

'Are you OK?'

'Yes. Yes.' Jack waved a dismissive hand in my general direction.

'What d'you think about VIMS being dismantled?' I asked.

'Your mum won't like it. But maybe it's the best thing.' To say that Jack's answer surprised me would be an understatement.

'What d'you mean?'

'I don't want your mum to be hurt any more.'

'Can't you fix it?'

'Some things can't be fixed.'

'But have you tried?'

Jack sighed and dropped his fork back onto his plate. 'Dominic, can we just leave it for tonight? I'm not in a very talkative mood.'

'I'm sorry.' I bowed my head. 'I think . . . I'll go to bed now.'

'OK. Leave your plate. I'll tidy everything away.'

After a final goodnight, I left Jack to it. In all the years I'd known him, I can't remember ever seeing him look so miserable.

Half an hour later, I'd cleaned my teeth and changed into my pyjamas. The house was deathly quiet. I wondered what Jack was doing. I couldn't hear a sound from downstairs. I lay in bed, determined not to fall asleep until I had thought of a way to stop Julie and Desica from dismantling Mum's project. If only my eyelids didn't feel quite so heavy . . .

The morning sun streamed through my window and onto my face. It woke me up. And it was as if it was trying to drum an idea into my head. I know that sounds fanciful, but the moment I opened my eyes, I knew what I had to do. Just like that. I had a quick shower and went in search of Jack. Surprise, surprise! He'd already beetled off to the hospital. He'd left a note on the front door.

Hi Dominic,

I'm sorry to disappear so early but I wanted to be with your mum. You can get yourself some cereal. The milk is

*in the fridge and the cereal is in the cereal cupboard! (I
can imagine your expression on reading the above!) I'll
phone you later. After breakfast, you're to go straight to
school and then come straight home again. Either I or
your granddad will come to pick you up and drive you
to the hospital. Avoid mischief and stay out of trouble!*

Love, Jack.

*P.S. And before you get in a huff and mumble about me
not being your dad yet, let me tell you that ever since
Carol and I started going out together, I've always
thought of you as my son.*

He really did know me well. I was just thinking that
very thing – about him bossing me around and not
being my dad yet – and here he'd written it down. I
smiled and took the note down off the door. With Jack
out of the way that left me free to carry out my plan.

I went into Mum's work room and linked up to the
VIMS unit. I didn't make one single mistake. I was a boy
on a mission. When at last the monitor screen flickered
into life, I got straight down to it.

'VIMS, this is Dominic Painter, Carol Painter's son
and I want you to listen carefully. VIMS, I want you to
leave the Desica building – low mode, maximum
stealth, silent running – and I want you to make your

way due south to Bailey's Point. VIMS, are you water-proof?'

'I am designed for mountainous, desert, land and submarine operations,' VIMS' monotone informed me.

After a quick think about it, I decided that submarine meant underwater, so he was.

'VIMS, do you have a internal map of how to get to Bailey's Point?'

'Yes.'

'Good. Then here's what I want you to do. VIMS, when you get to Bailey's Point, I want you to roll down the beach, making sure that no one sees you of course, and I want you to hide in the sea. VIMS, make sure you're completely covered by sea water and you're to wait in the sea until I give you further instructions. Is that clear?'

'I understand,' VIMS replied.

'VIMS, you're not to take orders from anyone else but me – OK? I'll give you a password. VIMS, the password is . . .' I racked my brains for a really good one. 'The password is "Have you heard the one about the painter, the decorator and the window cleaner?" Do you understand?'

VIMS didn't reply. It took me a couple of seconds to figure out why. I'm not at my best first thing in the morning.

'VIMS, repeat the password.'

'Have you heard the one about the painter, the decorator and the window cleaner?' VIMS asked in his deadpan voice.

'OK, VIMS, off you go – and remember, you're not to move or do anything until I or someone else gives you that password first.'

'Understood.'

I would've loved to stay and watch VIMS make it to Bailey's Point but it was over seven kilometres away from the Desica International building and I was already late for school. If I waited to make sure that VIMS got there safely, I'd get it in the neck from my teacher, then from Jack and my mum. Besides, I had every confidence that VIMS would get there. He didn't need me watching over him. *Him* . . . I gave a start of surprise. I'd started calling the thing – 'him'.

Switching off the computer system, I got down to the next most important task at hand – wolfing down my breakfast. As I chewed my wheat flakes, I tried to work out what I should do next. I had no doubt in my mind that in spite of all of Mum's precautions, the saboteur had still managed to get VIMS to ruin Mum's demo yesterday. Someone seemed desperate to make sure that the VIMS project didn't go any further. Or maybe I was looking at this the wrong way. Maybe it was more personal than that. What if someone was out to make sure that Mum got hurt? The thought turned my blood to ice water in my veins, but now that the idea was in my head I couldn't get it out. Did someone on Mum's project really hate her enough to do this to her? I shook my head. I couldn't believe it. Mum didn't have an enemy in the world.

But then I thought of her with that drip in her arm and linked up to all the monitors in her room, and somehow my conviction that Mum didn't have an enemy in the world rang false and hollow. So what now? How did I go about finding out who had done this to Mum? By the time I'd cleaned my teeth and left the house, I still didn't have the answer.

I didn't meet up with Liam on the way – which was kind of a surprise. I usually walked to school with him. I glanced down at my watch, then realized why I hadn't seen him. I was late. Not a little late but *really* late. Liam had probably set off for school, thinking I'd already left. As I approached the school gates, I must admit I was relieved to see that Matt Vinyl wasn't waiting for me. I'd missed everyone this morning. It was weird.

I set off around the grounds, looking for Liam. Unfortunately, I found what, or should I say who, I wasn't looking for. Matt and his cronies were deep in conversation against the far wall. Well, they could stay there as far as I was concerned. I immediately set off in the opposite direction. I decided to go to the library and wait for the bell to sound for registration and the first lesson. I'm not a coward, but I'm not stupid either. There was no point in hanging around just waiting for them to pick on me.

But I'd left it too late.

I heard my name and, turning round, I saw Matt and the others looking directly at me. I went hot all over and suddenly it was quite hard to breathe. I looked away and forced myself to walk at a slowish pace. I didn't want them to think that I was hurrying to get away from them, like I was scared of them or something.

'Dominic, stop!'

I turned to see them all come charging in my direction. It was like watching a herd of rhinos or elephants stampeding towards you, or a tsunami rushing up to sweep you away. I ran. I couldn't help it. Matt had a look of pure and utter hatred on his face and I knew I was in for a pounding. I had no idea why – and I didn't want to wait and find out either. But my leg started hurting and I was only three quarters of the way to the school entrance before I was surrounded. The next moment I was practically swept off my feet and pushed against the nearest wall. And there they all stood – Matt, Robert, Terry, Alan and Lawrence ('Don't call me Larry!').

'I know it was you,' Matt hissed at me.

I frowned at him but didn't speak.

'It *was* you, wasn't it?'

'What're you talking about?'

My shoulder got thumped. 'You threw that plant pot through my window, didn't you?' Spit flew out of Matt's mouth and splashed my cheek. But I didn't wipe it away. I was too busy staring at Matt, trying to figure out what he was saying. *What plant pot through his window?*

'That plant pot almost hit my sister. And you emptied our bin, didn't you? I know it was you.'

And all at once, it was crystal clear what he was talking about. I stared at him, astounded. For a brief second I wondered if I was dreaming, or maybe I was still running the VIMS simulation and all this was part of it. I wondered if I'd been swept somehow into a world of virtual reality (or was it virtual insanity!) – like Dorothy landing in Oz.

'Come on. Admit it.' Matt thumped me again.

'Leave him alone. I was in Dominic's house all evening. He didn't go anywhere.'

The mob parted slightly so that Matt could see who was speaking. Liam stood there. I tried to move away from the wall, but Robert pushed me back.

'You can't prove that,' Matt retorted.

'I don't have to,' Liam told him scornfully. 'Who do you think you are? Scotland Yard? Dominic and I were playing with his computer all evening until his grand-dad came to pick him up and take him to the hospital. His mum had an accident.'

'Don't tell him that.' I rounded on my friend. 'It's none of his business.' I turned to Matt. 'If someone chucked a plant pot through your window, then don't look at me. I didn't do it.'

Which I knew was technically but not morally the truth.

A frown of confusion crossed Matt's face as he stared at Liam. Then he turned back to me.

'I don't know how you did it, but I know it was you.'

'How on earth d'you think I picked up a great big wheelie bin and emptied it?' I flung at him.

His eyes narrowed. 'How d'you know we've got a wheelie bin?'

It took me a couple of seconds to work out that the throbbing, pounding sound I could suddenly hear was the sound of my heart trying to explode out of my chest.

'All the bins around here are wheelie bins.' Was it just to my ears that my voice sounded like a guilty squeak? I took a deep breath, then continued, 'I was just assuming that yours was too. And if you do have a wheelie bin, how on earth am I meant to have picked one of those things up and emptied it? And even if you have an ordinary bin, d'you really think I can pick one of those up and dump everything out of it? Or was it just kicked over?'

I was rambling. I knew it and yet I couldn't stop.

Don't let him suspect me! I repeated that thought over and over in my head.

'Er . . . what's going on here?' Miss Roy, one of the teachers, appeared from nowhere – and not a moment too soon.

'Nothing, miss,' Matt replied. 'We were just talking to Dominic here.'

'Is that the way you usually have a conversation?' Miss Roy frowned. 'With Dominic's back to the wall and all of you surrounding him like that?'

Matt and the others tried to shuffle backwards.

'Go and find something more constructive to do,' Miss Roy ordered. 'And I'll be keeping a close eye on all of you from now on.'

Only three terms too late, I thought.

After directing a bitter, suspicious look at me, Matt slunk off and his minions followed him like the sheep they were.

'Are you OK?' Miss Roy asked.

'I'm fine. We were just talking,' I told her.

Miss Roy took a long, hard look at me, but I didn't look away and I *think* I didn't look guilty. I can't have done, because she nodded and wandered off to sort out another fracas going on elsewhere.

Liam regarded me as I straightened up from off the wall.

'Well?'

'Well what?' I frowned.

Liam took a quick look around to make sure that there was no one within eavesdropping distance.

'I thought you said that VIMS was in simulation mode?'

'I thought he was,' I shrugged.

'Is that all you have to say?' Liam glared. 'You could've killed someone with that machine. You heard what Matt said about that plant pot only just missing his sister.'

'It wasn't my fault. I told you, I thought it wasn't real.'

'Well, it was real. Very real. And what're you going to do about it?'

'What would you like me to do about it?' I frowned. 'I can't go back in time and change things. Not even VIMS can do that.'

'That machine is dangerous,' Liam stated. 'It ought to be scrapped.'

'Who asked you?' I raged at him. 'And this is none of your business.'

I didn't need to bite his head off but it was too close to what Pops and Jack had been saying the night before.

'It is my business when you make me your accomplice,' Liam said, his voice giving me frostbite.

'I didn't make you an accomplice – at least not knowingly. Not deliberately.'

Liam gave me a sceptical look.

'That's the truth.'

'I wish I could believe you.' Liam shook his head. 'I think you knew that VIMS was really doing all that stuff.'

I stared at him. I couldn't believe what he'd just said and yet it was written on his face, as plain as day. Did he really believe that I would do something like that? Did he really think that I would get VIMS to hurl a plant pot through someone's window in real life – when it could hit anyone, a baby even? Obviously he did.

'If that's what you think, then I'm not going to argue with you.' I pushed past him.

'If you can get VIMS to do all that stuff in simulation mode, it's not that big a step before you can get him to do it for real.' Liam ran round me to block my way. 'After all, you never have to get your hands dirty.'

It was several seconds before I could trust myself to speak.

'Doing something as a game, a joke, something that you know isn't real, is a lot different to really doing it,' I told him. 'I can play lots of fighting or racing games on my computer at home, without wanting to go and pick a fight with the first person I come to, or steal a car and race down the High Street.'

'But this is different.' Liam looked a little less sure now – but the point is, he still said it.

'How is it different?' I asked bitterly. 'Because it's

Matt and VIMS and my chance to get even – and all from the comfort of my own home?'

He didn't answer.

'And d'you really think that if I was going to do something like that, I'd invite you along as a witness? D'you really think I'm that full of myself?'

Still no answer.

''Cause if you do, then go and tell Matt what I did. Go and tell the whole world.' And with that I pushed past him again and walked into the school building. I felt sick and furiously angry and something else that was much, much worse. My best friend had hurt me more than Matt and his cronies ever had or ever could.

Chapter Thirteen

Proof

Liam tried to talk to me more than once after that, but I just walked away from him. With Mum in hospital and Jack and Pops at her side and Liam thinking I could be as nasty as Matt, I felt alone and, yes, I admit it, very sorry for myself. As the day wore on, I found myself missing Mum more and more. And I began to regret giving Liam the cold shoulder. When I was away from him, I kept telling myself that the next time he tried to speak to me, I would answer, but when he did actually try to speak to me . . .

Let me give you an example!

'Oh, come on, Dominic! How many times do I have to say sorry?'

What I should've said was, 'Twenty million!' or, 'Once more with feeling!' or, 'OK, you've grovelled enough!'

But instead, I summoned up the dirty-filthiest look I could and walked away from him, my nose up in the air like there was a pongy smell under it. Silly, eh? But I couldn't get it out of my head that he thought I was some kind of monster. I guess the part of me that was hurt by his low opinion was bigger and stronger than the part of me that wanted to leave all the nastiness in the past. After lunch, he stopped trying to speak to me. I knew what that meant. If we were going to be friends again, then I was going to have to make the first move. Which of course made me resent him even more. Why should I be the first one to speak? Why should I apologize?

And that's how my school day ended. I walked home slowly, my whole body shrinking into itself like a folded-up telescope. For the first time, I couldn't think of anything funny or sarky to cheer myself up. Being in the right was very lonely. In a way, I was sorry I'd ever laid eyes on VIMS. I found I was sorry Mum had even had the idea to invent the rotten thing. It had caused nothing but TROUBLE. But I couldn't, I *wouldn't*, believe that there was something wrong with VIMS' programming. There couldn't be, not with Mum in charge.

'What you need to do,' the ideas part of me muttered, 'is prove that VIMS works!'

'Oh, is that all!' the sarcastic part of me replied.

Goodness only knows what passers-by must've thought when they heard me arguing with myself, but I'm always doing it!

I wondered if hiding VIMS in the sea had been a

smart move. I could only hope that I hadn't made things worse instead of better. Either way, I'd certainly complicated things. Had I been too hasty as far as VIMS was concerned? After all, Julie and Jack had only said that VIMS *might* be dismantled.

'Dominic! How are you? I was just on my way to the hospital to see your mum.'

I looked round to see Rayner, Mum's friend, driving alongside me.

'Oh, hi, Rayner,' I said without much enthusiasm.

'You mustn't worry about your mum.' Rayner stopped the car and jumped out, causing the car driving past him to swerve.

'Oops! Sorry!' Rayner called after the car.

Judging by the sign language the woman driver used, I don't think she was ready to accept his apology. Rayner ran over to me.

'So how are you really?' Rayner asked, ducking and weaving like he was in a boxing ring, his blond hair flip-flopping in his face as he moved. I was surprised he didn't just slide over the bonnet of his car and do fifty press-ups whilst he was talking to me. Rayner was totally hyperactive.

'Fifteen minutes in his company and I'm dog tired!' Mum always said.

'I'm OK,' I replied. I wished he would keep still before I got a crick in my neck.

'D'you want a lift to the hospital?'

'No. Jack said I was to go home first. He's going to pick me up there.'

'Are you sure?'

I nodded.

Rayner actually stopped dancing about for a moment, but it didn't last long.

'How's Monica?' I asked. Monica was his wife.

'She's fine.'

We both shuffled about in silence, searching for something to say.

'Would you really have Mum and Jack back at BFC Power if they wanted to leave Desica?' I asked.

'Like that!' Rayner snapped his fingers. 'And who knows, one day I might persuade your mum to come back.'

'What about Jack?'

'Jack!' Rayner snorted. 'Jack will never come back to BFC. Too many unhappy memories.'

At my puzzled look, Rayner continued, 'That's where Jack met his first wife, Alison.'

'Oh.' I hadn't known that. I knew that Jack and Alison hadn't had a happy marriage. I guess when Alison finally upped sticks and disappeared, Jack must've felt more relieved than anything else. The fact that he now wanted to marry my mum after a disastrous first marriage said even more about how much Jack cared for Mum.

'How are things at BFC anyway?' I asked. 'Are you still having problems?'

At Rayner's blank look, I continued, 'Mum said you were having problems in a section of your pipework at the power plant. Is that all sorted out now?'

Rayner sighed. 'I wish I could say it is, but no. Ever since we introduced our mechanical pigs a month ago, we've had nothing but trouble.'

'Your what?'

'Our pigs! It sounds funny, doesn't it?' Rayner laughed. 'They're little robots which move up and down the pipes checking for leaks and reporting faults. But the pigs monitoring sections A-5 to A-20 keep reporting problems that none of our other systems can verify. It's driving me crazy. The last thing I want is an explosion caused by a blockage.'

'So what're you going to do?'

'We'll just have to close down that section of the pipes and start digging. It's going to cost us a fortune and set us back months.'

'Oh, I'm sorry.'

'So am I!' he said. 'I was counting on your mum and her new super invention!'

'I think Mum was counting on you too,' I said.

'What d'you mean?'

'Mum's been having a hard time trying to sell the idea of VIMS recently. I think if VIMS could've solved the problems you've been having in your pipes, it would've been a great advertisement.'

'Well, there's no point in speculating about it now.' Rayner shrugged.

'I guess not! I'd better get going,' I told him. 'Jack is probably waiting for me at home.'

After waving bye to him, I turned to carry on walking home. And then it hit me! It was brilliant! Tremendous! STUPENDOUS!

'RAYNER!' I yelled, just as he was getting in his car.

He frowned at me. 'What's the matter?'

I beckoned him over. 'I've just had a great idea.'

'Oh yes?'

'What would you say if I told you I could get VIMS to the power plant and if you've got an access way leading to the pipes then he could find out what your problem is?'

'I thought your mum was still unconscious?'

'She is . . . as far as I know.'

'But you can operate VIMS?' Rayner asked.

'Yes, I can.'

'And you could get it to the power plant?'

'Yep!'

'And Desica would allow this?'

There he had me! I must've started to look really shifty then, because Rayner's eyebrows came down really low over his eyes as he said, 'Dominic . . .? What're you up to?'

'Who, me?'

'Yes, you!'

I thought about making up some plausible story but one wouldn't come to me, so I decided to tell the truth. Not the whole truth and nothing but the truth, but the truth nonetheless.

'Mum's got a remote control system at our home so I . . . er . . . I can direct VIMS from there. That's how come I can get it to BFC.'

'I take it Desica don't know anything about this.' Rayner hit the nail straight on the head.

'Not as such,' I admitted.

'I see . . .' Rayner actually stopped bopping about. He was weighing up the pros and the cons, the fors and the againsts, the yeses and the noes, the rights and the wrongs, the . . .

'So you'd send VIMS over to the power plant and let me use it?'

I nodded eagerly.

'Why?'

'Pardon?' I blinked, taken aback.

'Why would you want to do that?'

''Cause you need help to find out what's causing your mechanical pigs to malfunction. You want to make sure that nothing is happening that could cause an explosion,' I replied, playing his words back to him.

'And what's in it for you?' Rayner asked drily.

I smiled. No wonder Rayner was the manager of the power plant. Not much got past him!

'If VIMS sorts out your problem then it will also sort out Mum's problem at the same time,' I said.

'I'm not with you.'

'VIMS is in danger of being dismantled. A lot of people where Mum works think that VIMS is a waste of money, time and space – but it's not. And if VIMS solves your problems at the power plant then I get to prove it.'

'I see.'

And I could tell that he did see. The frown on Rayner's face deepened as he considered my proposal.

'Please, Rayner. I can't let them dismantle VIMS. Mum's worked too long and too hard on it. And it does work, I know it does. I just have to find some way to prove it.'

'I'll do it on one condition,' Rayner told me.

'Which is?'

'Your mum has to agree.'

'But Mum might still be unconscious . . .'

'That's the only way I'll do it, Dominic,' Rayner told me firmly.

He stood stock still to look at me directly, so I knew he was serious.

'OK,' I agreed reluctantly.

Rayner and I looked at each other. Was he thinking the same thing as me? I forced the thought out of my head. Mum was going to get better. She was.

Think of a joke, Dominic. Think of something funny, bizarre, sarcastic. Or don't think at all . . .

'Hi, Dominic.'

I turned my head and instantly smiled. 'Hi, Liam.'

And it was only after I'd spoken that I remembered I was meant to be mad at him.

'What're you doing?' Liam asked.

My smile faded. 'Going home.'

'Want some company?'

I considered. 'OK,' I said at last.

We started walking off together when I remembered Rayner. He drove past me with an understanding wave of his hand. I waved back.

'Who's that?'

'A friend of Mum's and Jack's,' I replied. 'He works at BFC Power just outside town.'

We walked on in silence.

'Look, I'm sorry . . .'

'I didn't mean . . .'

Liam and I spoke in unison. He looked at me and smiled. I smiled back.

'Sorry,' he said.

'That's OK.' I shrugged. And the funny thing is, it was OK. 'I don't want to lose a good friend over this.'

'Am I a good friend?' Liam asked, surprised.

I frowned at him. 'Of course you are.'

'I didn't know that,' Liam said thoughtfully.

'What d'you mean – you didn't know?'

'I thought you were going round with me as kind of a last resort, because you had no one else to go around with.'

I stared at him, my mouth opening and closing like a feeding goldfish. I wanted to tell him not to be so stupid, I wanted to ask him how he could think that, but the words wouldn't come.

'It's OK,' Liam shrugged. 'I know I don't have much going for me.'

'Don't talk rubbish. And OK, when Matt and I stopped being friends, maybe that is why I started talking to you,' I admitted. 'But that's not why I'm still talking to you. I think of you as my good friend – and I have done for ages. All right?'

Liam regarded me thoughtfully. Then he smiled. 'All right.'

'I should think so too,' I sniffed.

I was still a bit miffed at him, but I decided that I'd had more than my fair share of being miffed for one day.

'I'll walk you to your house if you like,' said Liam.

'Fine.' I tried to sound all casual about it as if it were no big deal – but it was really.

'Friends again?' asked Liam.

'We never stopped being friends,' I told him. And that was the truth.

'So how's your mum?'

I tried for a shrug which didn't quite work. 'I'm just praying she'll have woken up when I go to see her tonight,' I admitted. 'I hate this. I feel . . . I feel so guilty.'

'Guilty? About what?'

We carried on walking for a good minute before I could answer. To be honest, until the words had come out, I hadn't really realized that that was what I was feeling.

'Part of me wanted Mum to fail.' My voice grew quieter. 'She works all the time, especially since she had the VIMS idea. We never go anywhere or do anything. In fact over the last two years, I think I've seen more of Jack than my mum.'

'But that doesn't mean you wanted her to get hurt.'

'Yes, but—'

'No,' Liam interrupted emphatically, 'you never wanted her to get hurt so you've got nothing to feel guilty about.'

I sighed. I wanted so much to believe him but every move I'd made over the last few days had been a wrong step. So why should Mum's accident be any different?

'I don't know . . .'

'I do,' Liam said firmly. 'You may be a bit full of your-self sometimes and you may think you're always right and you may think your feeble jokes are all hilariously funny . . .'

'Get to the point,' I said. 'Any more unfailing support from you and I'll end up blubbing on the pavement!'

'But – as I was going to say before you interrupted me – you're OK,' Liam concluded in his typical underwhelming fashion.

'Thanks!'

'I mean it. You care about people and you're very loyal – and funny, when you're not trying to be.'

'Liam, I think I've heard enough now.'

Liam grinned at me. 'Just saying.'

'Just assassinating more like!'

Liam gave me a shove. 'Come on! Let's see who can tell the worst Matt Vinyl joke.'

'You're on.' This was a contest I could win, hands down.

Chapter Fourteen

Missing

As we walked home, Liam and I made up the very worst jokes we could about Matt Vinyl. Silly jokes like, 'What did Matt Vinyl do when he was told he had a flea in his ear? He shot it!' Or, 'Matt Vinyl asked me for ten pence to phone a friend. I gave him twenty pence so he could call all of them!' I told you they were silly! I told Liam a true but very painful joke.

'Matt was just about to thump me once when I said to him, "If frozen water is iced water, what is frozen ink?" Matt replied, "Iced ink." And I said, "You sure do!" Iced ink – I stink! Geddit?'

Liam groaned. 'How did Matt take that?'

'How d'you think? I got thumped.'

Liam looked at me like I'd lost my marbles. 'You're totally nuts. Matt is so jealous of you and your mum that he can hardly see straight, yet you keep on provoking him. It's one thing to defend yourself but it's something else entirely to go looking for trouble.'

'What d'you mean – he's jealous?'

'Your mum was never out of the papers around the same time that his mum ran off.' Liam shrugged. 'I guess that's why he started to . . . well, go a bit funny. And you made things worse by never shutting up about your mum. It was "My mum this!" and "My mum that!" '

My whole body went cold, as if I'd just been thrown into an icy swimming pool. 'I didn't. I didn't do that.'

'Of course you did. Which was only natural,' Liam said. 'You were proud of your mum. I would've been too. But I thought you could've handled Matt a little better.'

Stunned, I stared at Liam. Click! Click! Click! Click! It was like a whole load of jigsaw pieces falling into place in my head. How could I have been so *stupid*?

'I didn't realize,' I said at last.

Liam raised his eyes heavenwards. 'You must've been the only one in the class who didn't. Like I said, Dominic, sometimes you can be a bit too full of yourself.'

We carried on walking along in silence. It was as if I was looking at myself through new eyes or clearer glasses – and I wasn't too happy with what I saw. Was I really so self-centred that I hadn't realized why Matt had gone off me? Obviously, I was. I'd lost my friend and I knew I'd never get him back. Too much had passed between us now.

'Enough of Matt. He's too depressing,' Liam dismissed. 'What've you been up to recently? Anything exciting?'

I tried to make up my mind whether or not I should tell Liam about hiding VIMS. Something told me that he'd want me to order VIMS to go back to Desica.

'Penny for them?' Liam said.

'Huh?'

'Your thoughts.'

By this time we'd reached my house.

I shrugged. 'It's just that . . .' I paused at my front door, searching for the right words. I was so deep in thought that I didn't even notice the car parked outside my house, nor its occupant, until I heard the gate creak open.

'Dominic, hold on.' Julie came running up the garden path behind me.

'Is Mum . . . ?'

'Your mum's fine – as far as I know.'

Breathing a sigh of relief, I waited for Julie to continue.

'Dominic, I'm not going to beat about the bush. VIMS has disappeared.'

I was shocked. It's strange but true. I stared at Julie, totally stunned. All day I'd been waiting for the other shoe to drop. And drop it did – right on my head! Had I really thought that no one would notice a multi-million-pound piece of equipment going missing?

'Disappeared . . . ?' I whispered.

'Yes.' Julie's eyes narrowed. She looked from me to Liam and back again. 'D'you know anything about it?'

'What could I know?' I squeaked.

'You love your mum, don't you?' Julie asked.

The sudden unexpected question threw me.

'Of course I do.'

'And you'd do anything for her? Anything to make her happy?'

I gulped, trying to force down the rising tide of panic threatening to erupt at any second. *She knew* . . .

'I . . . er . . .'

'Dominic, this isn't the way to do it,' Julie said gently. 'I know you don't want to hurt Jack or your mum but if you know where Jack hid VIMS, you must tell me.'

'Pardon?'

'I know that Jack took VIMS and hid it somewhere.' Julie couldn't keep a hint of impatience from entering her voice. 'Dominic, you must tell me where he took the VIMS unit.'

'I don't understand . . .'

'Dominic, I'm not in the mood to play games. And this is a very serious and very dangerous game Jack is playing. Now, where is VIMS?'

123

A car pulled up behind Julie's white BMW. It was Jack. He was at my side in seconds flat.

'Is there a problem, Julie?' Jack asked.

'Jack, you can't get away with this. VIMS belongs to Desica, not to Carol and certainly not to you.'

'I've told you before and I'll tell you again, I have no idea what you're talking about,' Jack said icily.

'Right! That does it! You leave me no choice. If VIMS doesn't turn up by this time tomorrow then I'm going to have to call in the police.'

The police . . . Never in my wildest dreams had I thought that they'd get involved. After casting both of us a look that shrivelled, Julie strode back to her car and drove off without another word.

'Dominic, I'd better get home,' Liam said. 'Phone me later.'

I nodded. Jack and I watched as Liam set off up the road. He only lived round the corner but suddenly it was as if he lived on the other side of the world. I was beginning to realize how lucky I was to have Liam as my friend.

'Dominic, come into the house.' Jack put an arm around my shoulder as we both went inside.

'How's Mum? Is she OK?'

'She's still unconscious.'

'Oh . . .'

Jack closed the door behind us and we went into the

kitchen. I didn't need to ask him, just as he didn't need to say. Mum was seriously hurt. Perhaps more so than anyone had first thought if she still hadn't woken up.

'Can I go and see her?' I asked.

'Of course you can. We'll both go after we've had some dinner.'

'Have you been with her all day?'

'Since after lunch. I went into work this morning.' Jack searched through the fridge before taking out two microwaveable chicken and chips dinners.

'Does . . . does Julie really think you've done something to VIMS?' I couldn't meet his eyes when I asked that one.

Jack shrugged. 'VIMS has disappeared and, as far as Julie is concerned, I'm the obvious suspect.'

'Oh!' I stared down at the ground. Never had my shoe been so fascinating.

'So where is it, Dominic? What did you do with the VIMS unit?'

'Just because it's missing, doesn't mean that I—'

'Dominic, I didn't do it and neither did anyone else who works for your mum. Which leaves you.'

'But I don't know how . . .'

Jack raised his eyebrows at my attempted denial and it died on my lips.

'Where is it?'

'I hid it. I mean, I made him hide,' I admitted at last.

'That much I'd worked out for myself,' Jack said wryly.

'He's in the sea,' I muttered.

'He's *where*?'

'In the sea. I told him to stay there until I gave him the password.'

'Password? You made up a password?'

'Yes.'

Jack nodded slowly. 'Which is why he wouldn't respond to any of the commands we gave him from the control panel at Desica.'

'Jack, please understand. I had to. I couldn't let you dismantle Mum's work, I just couldn't.' The words came out in a frantic rush.

The microwave dinged to tell us that the food was ready, but I wasn't particularly hungry and I don't think Jack was either.

'What a mess!' Jack sighed. 'I don't know what to do for the best. I don't know . . .'

'Jack, you mustn't let anything happen to VIMS. You mustn't,' I pleaded.

'Sit down and eat your dinner,' Jack told me.

I picked at my food, my eyes more on Jack than on my plate. What was he going to do? Was he going to tell Julie what I'd done? Come to that, what was I going to do? I had to return VIMS or the police would be dragged into this and I might get Jack into trouble.

I certainly didn't want that.

'I'm going to have to return him, aren't I?' I said at last.

'I'm afraid so,' Jack replied.

'Can't I keep him for just one more day?' If I could just get him to the power plant . . .

'No, Dominic. You heard Julie, she's going to call the police. Your mum's got far too much on her plate already without worrying about the two of us down at the local police station trying to explain what we're doing with a multi-million-pound robot.'

The two of us . . . I smiled at Jack, grateful for the way he'd said 'we' and 'us'. And in that moment, I felt like Jack was really and truly my dad. And then I sighed, because I knew he was right. I was going to have to return VIMS before I got us both in serious trouble.

'All right. I'll tell VIMS to go back to Desica tonight,' I said. 'But can we go and see Mum first?'

Chapter Fifteen

Permission

When we walked into Mum's side room at the hospital, Pops turned to us, his eyes ablaze.

'She woke up. Carol woke up!'

I was at her side in an instant. 'Mum? Mum, it's me, Dominic.'

'I think she just fell asleep again,' Pops told me. But that didn't stop me.

'Mum? Mum, are you all right?'

Her eyelids fluttered open. 'Dominic?'

'Mum!' I tried to hug her but it was a bit difficult so I kissed her on the cheek instead. 'You smell just like a hospital bed pan!'

'Charming!' Mum said indignantly. Her eyes were wide awake now.

'A clean one,' I hastened to assure her. 'And you smell of tonsil sticks and antiseptic.'

'That's even worse.' Mum glared.

'No, I didn't mean that you smelt . . .'

'Dominic, quit whilst you're behind,' Jack suggested.

I shut up. That'd come out entirely wrong! I'd only meant that she smelt of hospitals and medicine.

'Mum, how're you feeling?'

'I've been better.' Mum smiled, then winced. 'And it hurts when I breathe.'

'That's 'cause you had a punctured lung and a broken rib,' Jack told her.

'I know. The doctor told me,' Mum sighed.

'Mum, I need to talk to you.'

'Go on then.' Mum closed her eyes momentarily. She looked exhausted, and worse than that, so fragile.

'I don't think your mum's up to a long discussion now,' said Jack, his expression sombre.

'It won't take long. Please, D . . . Dad?'

Jack gave a start of surprise. He looked at me, a smile spreading across his face.

'I like the sound of that,' he said softly.

'So do I,' Mum grinned.

'So do I,' I said. 'So can I talk to Mum?'

'Go on then,' Jack said reluctantly.

I regarded him and Pops. 'Can I talk to Mum *alone*?'

That really threw them. Jack opened his mouth only to snap it shut a moment later. He wanted to ask me what I was going to talk about. He left the question unasked but floating in the air between us. I wasn't going to say anything else – at least, not until Mum and I were alone.

'Don't upset your mum, OK?' Jack said at last.

I nodded.

'What're you up to, Dominic?' Pops said suspiciously.

I just smiled at him.

Finally they left the room.

'What's the matter?' Mum asked me the moment the door was closed.

'Mum, I saw Rayner today.'

'So did I,' said Mum. 'He bought me those flowers.'

'Yes! Yes!' I dismissed impatiently. 'The thing is, Julie's talking about dismantling VIMS . . .'

'What? She can't.' Mum struggled to sit up, only to groan heavily and lie back down again.

'Mum, are you all right?'

'I think so.'

I didn't. Her face had gone ashen. She was obviously in a great deal of pain.

'Mum, don't be so silly. Lie down,' I told her sternly.

'They can't dismantle VIMS. I won't let them,' Mum fumed.

'I thought you might feel that way about it, so I . . . I . . .'

Mum's eyes narrowed. 'Keep going!'

'I used the remote control system in our house to hide VIMS in the sea at Bailey's Point.' I closed my eyes and lowered my head as I waited for the storm to descend around me.

Silence. I opened first one eye, then the other.

'Not a bad idea!' Mum said.

My eyes popped out then. 'You mean it? I thought you were going to go ballistic.'

'Well, you only hid it to stop Julie from wrecking years of my hard work.' Mum gave a slight shrug. 'I probably would've done the same thing myself.'

'Phew!' I breathed. 'The trouble is, Julie is threatening to phone the police and Jack says I have to tell VIMS to go back to the testing area at Desica.'

'Hhmm!'

'That's not all,' I admitted.

'I'm listening.'

'I saw Rayner earlier when he was on his way here to see you. I thought that if we could use VIMS to sort out the pipe problems at the power plant then we could prove that VIMS is useful and not dangerous. I know it knocked you over and . . .'

'Forget that.' Mum waved that aside. 'That wasn't his fault. I obviously didn't find all the sabotaged code in his system.'

'So what should I do about VIMS and Rayner? If there's still bad code in VIMS' system then I can't send it over to BFC. It might hurt someone else.'

'VIMS needs to go back to Desica but we need some way of locking everyone else out of his system until I'm on my feet again.'

'Well, I've given VIMS a password and told him that he's not to accept any commands at all without being given the password first.'

Mum grinned at me. 'Dominic, you're a genius!'

'I take after my mum then,' I said modestly.

Mum took hold of my hand, which was really soppy. And even soppier, I didn't pull away or tell her to let go. There aren't many times when it's just Mum and me and no one else.

'Oh, and thanks for calling Jack "Dad",' Mum said. 'He'd never say anything, but it means a lot to him.'

'It means a lot to me too. I like him very much.'

'Which is just as well!' we both said in unison.

'Right then. Here's what you do,' Mum said, her tone suddenly brisk and business-like. 'Send VIMS back to Desica, but make sure that no one can do a thing to him without the password. No downloading or uploading of code, no commands, no nothing. Understood?'

I nodded. 'And what about Jack? Should I tell him . . .?'

'No. Jack is a "play it safe and by the book" man and this is not one of those times. Besides . . .'

The door opened.

'Dominic, that's enough. I don't want Carol to get over-tired,' Jack insisted.

'I've finished anyway,' I told him.

'Jack, you stay here with Carol. I'll take Dominic home,' said Pops.

'Are you driving or are we taking a bus?'

'We're driving.' Pops frowned.

My face fell.

'And what's the matter with my driving, young man?' Pops said with indignation.

'You drive at two miles an hour and like you're the only one on the road,' I told him straight. 'You always manage to cheese off everyone around you.'

'Cheesing people off – it's what I live for!' Pops winked.

I shook my head. So much for grown-ups behaving in a grown-up manner. Pops was terrible!

'Come on. Out with it, you two. What's the decision? Is Dominic going to send VIMS back to the testing centre or not?' Jack asked.

'How did you know . . . ?' Mum began. Then she smiled. 'Jack, my love, you are too smart for your own good!'

I left them making lovey-dovey goo-goo eyes at each other. Pops and I headed home.

'I'll see you later, Dad?'

Jack turned to me with a smile. 'Yes. I'll see you later, son.'

Chapter Sixteen

New Orders

I was right about Pops' driving. I kept my eyes closed for most of the journey to avoid the dirty looks and the expressive hand gestures of the other drivers on the road. At last the car stopped.

'We're home now. You can open your eyes,' Pops said.

I looked around gingerly, just in case Pops was winding me up. But he wasn't. We were home at last.

'Pops, no offence, but next time can we take the bus?'

'Humph! Now d'you see why I prefer to drive with no one else in the car?'

'I think everyone else would prefer it if you drove that way as well,' I told him.

I hopped out of the car, expecting Pops to come out too but he stayed behind the wheel.

'Aren't you coming in?' I asked.

'It's my bingo night tonight. You'll be all right by yourself for a couple of hours, won't you?'

' 'Course I will. Go and enjoy yourself. I know how you old people love bingo!'

'I am not old,' Pops sniffed. 'And I'll have you know we have all sorts of people at bingo – young and old.'

'And sad and boring!'

'Watch it!'

I slammed the door shut and watched as Pops took off down the road like a snail in a hurry. It would take a good half an hour before he got that annoyed look off his face. I'd barely set foot through the front door when the phone started ringing. It'd been all go today and no mistake. And it wasn't over yet.

'Hello?'

'Dominic, this is Ja— I mean, Dad. Your mum told me what the two of you were talking about.'

'I thought she might.'

'I want you to send VIMS directly back to Desica. He is not to go to the power plant first – d'you understand?'

'Yes, Dad.'

'I mean it. I'm working on a plan to flush out the saboteur, so I want VIMS back in the testing area as soon as possible. Do not send him to BFC. Do not send him anywhere else either.'

'Do not pass Go! Do not collect two hundred pounds! I hear you!'

'Good. Send him back to Desica then switch off the remote control system. OK?'

'OK.'

'See you later, Dominic.'

Frowning, I put the phone down. Jack was adamant about what I had to do. I wondered what his plan was. He wasn't going to have much luck doing anything with VIMS while I was the only one who knew the password. Should I phone him up and tell him so? No, he'd phone back if he needed it and I didn't want to interrupt his time with Mum. I made my way upstairs to Mum's work room. My leg was beginning to hurt quite badly and I suddenly felt so tired. I guess it was a reaction to everything that had happened in the last few days. After VIMS was safely back at Desica, I'd have an early night.

After switching on the remote system, I put on the gloves and the visor and began.

'VIMS, have you heard the one about the painter, the decorator and the window cleaner?'

VIMS' viewer switched on. I only knew that because the quality of the blackness on the screen changed. It went from a solid black to a wavy, inky blackness.

'VIMS, head back to Desica, low mode, maximum stealth, silent running.'

A minute later, VIMS emerged from the sea. It was dark now, but there was a full moon so I could make out the cliffs and the parts of the beach. I took off the VR glove but left on the visor. VIMS didn't need my help until he got back to Desica and even then I was sure he could now work out how to open door handles without my help. After all, he was an artificial intelligence system who was meant to learn about his environment and the things around him as he used them – or so Mum had said.

I closed my eyes and tried to drift away from the pain in my leg. Once in a while it really started to play up and then I'd be in agony for about half a day before it would ease off again. I could tell I was in for one of those bouts. My ankle joint was hurting and there were shooting pains running up and down my calf.

I must have nodded off for a while, because when I opened my eyes I was shocked to find myself in the middle of our town. Eyes like dinner plates, I stared at the scene around me. Had I been sleepwalking? And only then did I remember that I still had the visor on and I was seeing images relayed back by VIMS, not images of what was actually around me.

I took off the visor to look up at the clock on the wall. I couldn't believe it. I'd been asleep for almost an hour. I must've been more tired than I thought. I put the visor back on before rubbing my sore calf. Then I remembered something. In giving VIMS the password, I'd put him back into normal mode where anyone from Desica could give him a command.

'VIMS, have you received any commands over the last forty minutes?'

'Yes,' came the monotone reply. 'Two.'

For a moment, even my blood froze in my body. Someone had given VIMS two commands whilst I'd nodded off. 'VIMS, the password is "Have you heard the one about the painter, the decorator and the window cleaner?" You're not to accept any more commands until you hear that password. VIMS, do you understand?'

'Yes.'

'What commands were you just given?'

'Proceed to Desica at new co-ordinates. Secure the area. Defcon 1.'

From the look of it, VIMS was still heading back to Desica, so I was OK.

'VIMS, who gave you those orders?'

'The orders were typed in from the command console at Desica,' VIMS replied.

Which meant it could've been anyone.

'VIMS, do you know who input the commands?'

'The commands were input from the Resnick account.'

Resnick . . . Julie Resnick! I couldn't believe it. *Julie* . . . She was the one responsible for sabotaging Mum's project? But why? It didn't make any sense. What could she possibly hope to gain by doing such a thing? I couldn't get my head around it.

I put the visor down and limped downstairs for a painkiller for my leg, still pondering on what VIMS had told me. My leg was still playing up but at least the pains in my calf had settled down and, while they weren't getting any better, they weren't getting any worse either. I went into the kitchen. My thoughts slid back to VIMS and Julie. There was only one thing to do. I'd make sure that VIMS had proof of what Julie had done before I started hurling accusations around. There was something else that was troubling me.

Secure the area . . . Defcon 1 . . . What did that mean? Maybe it meant that when VIMS got back to Desica he had to go down to the testing area and make sure everything was secure? It didn't sound right. I poured myself half a glass of water and dropped a soluble painkilling tablet into it. Whilst I was waiting for it to dissolve, I decided that I'd think better with a Southern Fried chicken leg in my mouth and I started rummaging through the fridge. Eureka! I was in luck. There was one left. I took out the chicken leg and, after drinking down the painkiller, I made my way back upstairs to the work room. VIMS should've reached Desica by now. I put on the visor.

CRRAAASSSSHHH!

Glass exploded into the room and showered me like rain. I shook my head frantically to get the shards out of my hair. I took off my visor to see what on earth had happened. And then I saw him – VIMS. And he was heading straight towards me, his arms outstretched. I stared, frozen. His hands got closer and closer, his fingers like the ends of a Swiss Army knife revolving on the disc-like mounting. That was the only sound in the room – the whirring of the disc and the tools that were his fingers clicking as they stretched out towards me. And only when I could smell the metal beneath my nostrils did my mind start working again. I turned and ran – at least I tried to. My leg chose that moment to try and seize up altogether. I tried to head for the stairs, but the pain in my leg told me there was no way I could go down them fast enough – not without VIMS catching up with me first. At the last moment, I turned and scrambled for my bedroom. My leg was a dead weight I had to drag behind me but for each one step that I took, VIMS took two, clunking his way towards me, his arms outstretched. I clambered onto my bed underneath my window. I searched for a place in my room to hide, but I was too late. VIMS was in the doorway. With a whimper of fear, I shoved my bedroom window open and tried to make it out onto the conservatory roof, but now my legs weren't work-ing at all. And at last it fell into place. Too late I under-stood VIMS' new commands. Too late I realized what 'new co-ordinates' and 'secure the area' meant. VIMS was going to 'deal' with me – and I wasn't going to survive.

Chapter Seventeen

Rescue

'VIMS, over here. Behind you,' Jack screamed out from the landing. I was too petrified to even turn my head to look at him. Out of the corner of one eye I could see him waving his hands above his head to attract VIMS' attention.

VIMS took another step towards me. One of his feet was now on my bed. The mattress groaned under his weight. One more step and he would reach me. I sat back even further, trying to push my back through the wall behind me.

'VIMS, come and get me,' Jack shouted.

VIMS halted in his tracks. The dome that was his head spun round. I couldn't see Jack now. I could see nothing but VIMS, standing before me, just a heartbeat away from ripping me apart. Something hit VIMS on the back of the head. VIMS backed away from me and stepped off the bed before rolling over the object that had hit him. I glanced down without moving my head. It was a towel.

VIMS carried on rolling out of the door. He was after Jack now. He'd obviously assessed him as the bigger threat. And once he had dealt with Jack, he would be back for me . . .

'Dominic, what's the password?' Jack shouted frantically.

I opened my mouth, but the words wouldn't come.

'Dominic! Quick! The password,' Jack called.

If I didn't do something – and fast – Jack would be killed. I couldn't let that happen. I couldn't. I sprang off the bed and ran after VIMS and Jack.

'VIMS, have you heard the one about the painter, the decorator and the window cleaner? VIMS, stop!'

I cursed myself for inventing such a stupid password. At the time I'd thought I was being so clever. Jack ran into Mum's bedroom. He tried to slam the door shut behind him but VIMS shoved it open. Jack fell to the floor and immediately started scrambling backwards. VIMS drew himself up to his full height, totally over-whelming and overpowering. He took a step forwards. He raised his other foot, ready to bring it down on Jack's chest. Jack was against the wall. There was nowhere else to run.

'VIMS, HAVE YOU HEARD THE ONE ABOUT

THE PAINTER, THE DECORATOR AND THE WINDOW CLEANER? VIMS, STOP!'

Please don't let anything happen to Dad, I prayed. Please let him be all right.

'VIMS, STOP NOW. STOP!'

VIMS' leg moved downwards. He was going to crush Jack. But then the leg slowed and stopped, freezing just a few centimetres above Jack's chest. Jack immediately rolled out from beneath VIMS' foot.

'Dad, are you OK?'

I ran into the room. Jack was breathing heavily, a horror-stricken look on his face. His eyes were wide open and it was as if they'd been welded that way. Neither of us said a word for several moments.

'Dominic, are you OK?' Jack whispered at last.

I found that I couldn't speak, so I shook my head instead. It'd be a long time before I was OK again.

Jack came over to me and hugged me. 'I never want to go through that again,' he said. 'I thought we'd both had it!'

'Thanks for saving my life, Dad.' The words came out in a cough. I pulled away from Jack, embarrassed.

'Thank *you* for saving my life,' Jack returned. He turned to VIMS. 'VIMS, security override A-4-27R. VIMS, shut down.'

VIMS' leg moved downwards to touch the ground.

Then he folded in on himself until he was no more than a box on the ground. But I didn't even have to close my eyes to remember how he'd looked when he was coming for me. Relentless and terrifying.

'Are you sure you're OK?' Jack asked again.

I nodded.

'If anything had happened to you . . .' Jack actually shuddered. 'Why on earth did you re-activate the password on VIMS?'

'I . . . I thought it would be safer until he got back to Desica,' I whispered.

'I had to drive like a bat out of hell to get here,' Jack said grimly. 'I thought I'd be too late . . .'

'Why did she do it?'

'Pardon?'

'Julie Resnick. Why did she reprogram VIMS to come here? Why did she want to hurt me?'

'What d'you mean?'

'She gave VIMS a new set of co-ordinates so that he would come here instead and she told VIMS to secure the area. That's why he kept coming after me.'

'I see.'

'We should call the police,' I said. My voice was getting stronger now, and with each passing second, so was my fury.

'No,' said Jack thoughtfully. 'Leave Julie to me.'

'What're you going to do?'

'I'm going to finish this, once and for all,' Jack said.

And there was a grimness in his voice, a determination that told me Julie wasn't going to get away with trying to hurt me or my mum. Jack was going to see to that.

Chapter Eighteen

Mum in Charge

When I woke up the following morning, I got the shock of my life. No, I take that back. What had happened the night before was the biggest one. So I'll change that to I got the second biggest shock of my life. Mum was home. I should've realized when I awoke to the smell of bacon and toast. Dad was strictly a cereal and fruit juice man.

'Mum, what're you doing here?' I asked, stunned.

'What does it look like?' Mum asked. 'I'm making some breakfast and then you, me and VIMS are going to the power plant.'

'What for?'

'To prove that VIMS isn't dangerous, of course. To prove that he can do exactly what I said he could do.'

An image of VIMS, tall and menacing as he'd been the previous night, flashed in my head. VIMS *was* dangerous – as dangerous as the person who issued his commands. His actions could be dictated by the person controlling him. And if that person was a serious nutter like Julie, then look out!

'Does Rayner know about this?' I asked at last.

'I phoned him late last night. He's already at the plant, waiting for us.'

'On a Saturday?'

'The power plant runs twenty-four hours a day, seven days a week,' Mum informed me. 'So why not on a Saturday?'

I bet Rayner's wife Monica loves you for dragging Rayner out of the house on a Saturday, I thought – but I decided to keep the thought to myself. I toyed with the idea of telling Mum what had happened the night before, but Dad had said he wanted to tell Mum himself – in his own way and in his own time so that it wouldn't make her do anything silly. From the look of it, he was too late.

'Where's Dad?' I asked, looking around. This was one of those times when I knew I wouldn't be able to talk any sense into Mum at all. This was definitely a job for Jack.

Mum frowned. 'I don't know what's happened to him. I must admit I was expecting to see him when I arrived here.'

'I can't believe the hospital let you out so quickly,' I said, shaking my head. 'I know there's a shortage of beds but this is ridiculous.'

'They didn't exactly let me out,' Mum mumbled.

'Then what did they do – exactly?'

'I discharged myself.'

'You did what?' I said, astounded. 'Why would you do anything so stupid?'

'You sound just like Jack,' Mum said defensively.

'So you have seen him this morning . . .' I asked, confused.

'I haven't,' Mum denied. 'But if he was here, that's exactly what he would be saying!'

'Mum, you have to go back to hospital.'

'No, what I have to do is stop Julie from dismantling VIMS,' said Mum, holding her side. 'Besides, I only had concussion and that's gone now and my side only hurts when I laugh – and believe me, I'm not in a laughing mood. I have to stop Julie before it's too late.'

It's already too late, I thought. And Julie had moved beyond just ruining VIMS. For some reason she was now out to get me. Was it because I hadn't told her where VIMS was? Or was it her way of trying to get Jack to toe the line? 'Mum, VIMS is upstairs.'

'Upstairs?' Mum stared at me. 'What's he doing up there?'

'It's a long story,' I sighed.

'I'm all ears.'

'Dad said he'd tell you.'

Breakfast was forgotten as Mum tried to dash out of

the room, although a quick grunt of pain soon put paid to that. Holding onto the banister, she went up the stairs as fast as she could. VIMS was in the house. Everything else could wait.

'He's in your bedroom,' I told her.

Mum fussed and clucked over him for ages. I was surprised that she didn't try to tickle him under his metal chin! Mum made for her work room to switch on the remote system.

'Er . . . Mum, there's something I should tell you . . .'

Mum opened the work-room door. 'What on earth . . . ?' She stared when she saw the room and the window. Jack had taped cardboard across it as best he could, but it was a real mess. Mum turned to glare at me.

'I didn't do it. VIMS did,' I protested.

'Just what's been going on here?'

'Dad said—'

'That he'd tell me. Yes, so you keep saying.' Mum frowned.

I wasn't going to argue with her. I stayed close by while Mum activated VIMS. And I kept VIMS at a respectable distance. I felt uncomfortable even being in the same building with the thing. Last night, Dad had told me more than once that now it was shut down, VIMS was perfectly safe. Dad had even used the remote system to ensure that when VIMS was reactivated, it would be under the control of the remote system only until that command was specifically changed. That way Julie couldn't issue any more commands from the control panel at Desica.

'Dominic, VIMS is safe, I promise you,' he told me. 'I wouldn't let anything happen to you or your mum.'

And whilst I believed Dad, somehow I still didn't quite trust it. Last night, it had only done what it'd been programmed to do but . . . But. I also realized with a start that I'd gone back to calling VIMS 'it'.

I sat down behind Mum. Ten minutes later, her hands were still moving like greased lightning across the keyboard as she fiddled with VIMS' programming.

'What're you doing?'

'Just isolating some code that's been changed in the last couple of days. I'll work out who changed it later after the test at the power plant.'

'I know who changed the code,' I told Mum. 'It was Julie Resnick.'

'Julie?' Mum gave a start of surprise. 'Why d'you say that?'

'VIMS told me.'

'He did? That's interesting . . .'

'You don't sound very put out about it,' I said. And she didn't. Her tone was thoughtful rather than angry.

'Come on, Mum. Share! Why're you so calm about the fact that Julie is the saboteur?'

'I'm not convinced she is,' Mum told me at last.

'But VIMS said—'

'VIMS said what he was programmed to say,' Mum interrupted. 'The saboteur has been covering his or her tracks like a real expert. So why get careless now? It's all a bit too convenient.'

'Maybe Julie slipped up and forgot to cover her tracks?' I suggested.

'Possible, but very unlikely,' Mum dismissed.

And now I'd had a chance to think about it, I agreed with Mum. 'So you think someone was just trying to put the blame on Julie?'

'It looks that way to me,' said Mum. 'But at the moment, my first priority is to get VIMS to the power plant and to prove once and for all that VIMS works as he should. If everything goes well then Rayner can give me a lot of good publicity.'

'And that will make it harder for Desica to shut you down.'

'Exactly.' Mum smiled. 'Now I've re-routed a couple of his command pathways so that he should bypass the changed code and behave himself.'

'Are you going to the power plant now?'

'Yep. And you're coming with me.'

'I am?'

'I'm not up to fetching and carrying at the moment. I'll need your help,' said Mum. 'I'll leave a note for Jack telling him where we're going. If he gets back in time, he can catch up with us there. Help me load the remote control unit into the car.'

It didn't take too long to load up the car. VIMS was the most bother. Mum had to put on the VR visor and gloves and direct VIMS to climb up into the boot of our car, then fold itself up. As it moved through the house, I kept a wary eye on it and didn't get too close. I thought more than once about telling Mum what'd happened the night before, but Dad had stressed that he wanted to be the one to explain everything to Mum.

Within half an hour, Mum was driving us to the power station. After the first couple of miles, Mum got me to change gear whilst she pressed down on the clutch pedal. I could only hope that we didn't get spotted by the police. And although I was sitting next to her in the passenger seat, I spent most of my time glancing behind me to make sure VIMS wasn't trying to enter the car from the boot or something. Every time Mum turned a corner she winced or flinched so that by the time we reached the power station, I knew she was in a lot of pain.

'Mum, you should be in hospital,' I told her. 'Dad's going to hit the roof when he realizes what you've done.'

'He'll understand.'

'He'll still be as mad as a whacked wasp at you.'

152

Mum started laughing at that, only to stop abruptly and hold her side.

'Mum, this is silly. It can wait a couple more days, can't it?'

'No. It's now or never,' Mum insisted. 'I need to buy some time and this will do it for me. I took some painkillers so I'll be able to manage for another couple of hours.'

'You took some painkillers?' I asked. 'But look at the state of you. You should be in hospital.'

'Dominic.' Mum looked me straight in the eyes. 'Give it a rest!'

So with a heavy huff and a pouty puff, I shut up!

At the power plant's security gate, a beefy guard in a grey uniform stepped forward. 'Can I help you?'

'Er . . . yes. We're here to see Rayner Alten. He's expecting us.'

'Just a moment.' The guard went back to his little cubby hole and picked up the phone. We had to wait over a minute before he put it down and walked back to us.

'Drive up to the main building, then turn left and carry on for about a quarter of a mile to the maintenance building A to D.'

As Mum drove off, I asked, 'How big is this place anyway?'

'Huge.' Mum stated the obvious. 'And the pipework

and cabling under this place stretches out for hundreds of kilometres.'

I whistled appreciatively. I'd had no idea it was that vast. Rayner was bobbing about, waiting for us outside a huge bungalow-type building as we pulled up. He waved and immediately ran over.

'This is great, Carol!' he grinned when Mum was barely out of the car. 'You are really helping me out here.'

Rayner and Mum kissed each other. Rayner was weaving about so much I was surprised he didn't end up kissing the back of Mum's head instead.

'We're helping each other.' Mum smiled. 'I'm going to have VIMS record everything he does and we can play the tape back to the board at Desica.'

'Will you get into trouble for this?' Rayner asked.

'Probably,' Mum said. 'But it'll be worth it. I'll save my creation!'

'And I'll save the power plant thousands of pounds if VIMS can find out what the problem is.'

'Then let's get cracking.' Mum smiled again.

Rayner and I carried the virtual reality equipment into the main control room of the building – what Rayner called the Operating Room. And the room was huge. They certainly believed in doing everything on a big scale at the power plant. There were monitors and different types of computers as far as the eye could see.

The noise of the fans and the machinery in the room was uncomfortably loud. I hoped what we had to do wouldn't take longer than a couple of hours, otherwise we'd all end up with raging headaches.

Mum brought in the CD disks which contained all of VIMS' remote control programs. We had to wait until Mum had downloaded the programs onto one of the plant's computers and made sure everything was working before she could put on the VR visor and glove and direct VIMS out of the boot of our car and into the building.

'Actually, I've had a better idea,' Mum said once VIMS was outside the Operating Room. 'Rayner, I want you to command VIMS. That way, no one can say it's a set-up on my part.'

'But I don't know how . . .'

'That's OK. It's really simple,' said Mum. 'It'll only take me twenty minutes to take you through it.'

Whilst Mum was showing Rayner how to issue commands and how to operate VIMS, I wandered off to look at VIMS through the glass door. It just sat there, looking back at me. It didn't look particularly frightening or menacing now. It stood perfectly still, folded up on itself. Just a few days ago I'd thought it the most miraculous, wonderful thing I'd ever seen. But now it almost gave me the creeps. A frown tightened over my lips as I regarded VIMS with growing loathing. It really had been nothing but trouble. Still, this was its chance to redeem itself.

'VIMS, don't mess this up,' I mouthed at it.

'OK, Dominic, we're ready to go,' Mum called out a little later.

I walked back to Rayner and Mum, eager to begin.

'The lifts that allow access to the pipes are in the small machine room across the hall,' Rayner told us. 'So I'll direct VIMS there first.'

Rayner issued his commands with confident ease. He forgot to say VIMS at the beginning of a couple of his commands, but that was about the only thing he got wrong. I glanced across at the glass door, just in time to see VIMS turn and trundle off.

It was a long process after that. VIMS had to go into a tiny lift which took it down and down and down towards the underground pipes.

'That lift is how we get the mechanical pigs down to the pipes,' Rayner explained. 'It's too dangerous down there for people. If we did send someone down there, we'd have to shut down the power plant or at least a major section of it. That's why VIMS is ideal for this.'

When at last VIMS did reach the pipes, Rayner consulted another computer with what looked like blueprints on the screen.

'What's that?' I asked.

'That's a diagram of all the pipes and access tunnels

down below us,' Rayner told me. 'I want VIMS to carry out a systematic search of each pipe in the Alpha section.'

Rayner began. He directed VIMS up one pipe and then down another. Turn left, turn right, straight ahead, turn round. On and on it went, until I don't know about VIMS but my head was certainly swimming. I looked at the monitor which showed us what VIMS was seeing, but apart from pipework and tunnel walls there wasn't anything else to see. The pipes must've been about ninety centimetres across and some of them were much, much bigger, but believe me, when you've seen one pipe, you've seen them all.

'Rayner Alten to the phone please. Rayner Alten to the phone.' A man's voice boomed out over the tannoy, making me jump.

'What's the matter now?' Rayner grumbled.

He pulled off the glove and visor and handed them to Mum before heading for the nearest phone. Mum continued to direct VIMS through the pipes and tunnels, carefully following the schematic on Rayner's computer. I watched as Rayner stuck a finger in his ear whilst holding the phone to the other ear.

I could see rather than hear him say, 'Pardon? Pardon? What?'

Then he started talking into the phone and I couldn't lip read any more.

'How're we doing, Mum?' I asked.

Mum was looking at the monitor before her. The image VIMS was playing back to us was of yet more tunnel walls.

'Nothing so far,' Mum sighed.

Rayner came over. 'Jack's here – and he's none too pleased with either of us. I didn't realize you'd discharged yourself from hospital, Carol.'

'You're not going to nag me, are you?' Mum pleaded.

'I think you're about to get all the nagging you can handle. Jack is driving here now.'

'So where is he? At our house?'

'No, he's at the security gate.'

Mum sighed. I think she was hoping to have a bit longer before Dad arrived to have a rant at her.

Rayner smiled wryly at the expression on Mum's face. 'Any progress?'

'None so far.'

'Jack's going to make you go back to hospital,' I told Mum smugly. 'And quite right too. You shouldn't have left.'

'Dominic, darling . . .'

'Yes, I know – shut up!' I finished Mum's sentence for her.

'Not the words I would've used but . . .'

'But the meaning's the same!' I smiled.

'Let me have a try again,' Rayner asked.

Mum took off her visor and was just about to take off the VR glove when we heard VIMS' voice.

'Obstruction found,' it said.

We all turned to look at the monitor. The three of us gasped in total horror. There on the screen, we could see . . . a body.

Chapter Nineteen

The Truth

A body . . .

I couldn't believe it. I turned to Mum, thinking my eyes must be playing tricks. But Mum's expression looked to be a mirror image of my own. She had the same astounded look on her face.

'A body?' she whispered. 'It can't be. There must be some kind of mistake. Either that or it's a sick joke . . .'

Both Mum and I turned to Rayner, but he was absolutely still and staring at the screen.

'Rayner . . . ?'

'This is no joke,' Rayner said grimly. 'It really is a body.'

The person had their back to us but I could see it was a woman with light-coloured hair and wearing a blue dress. My stomach churned horribly. I had to take several deep breaths before it began to quieten down. A *body* . . .

'How did a body get down there?' Mum whispered.

'It must've been put in there when the pipes were laid years ago. There's no way a body could get down there and that far into the tunnels now.' Rayner's expression was stony.

'But it doesn't look like it's been down there for years and years.' I shook my head. 'It's not a skeleton.'

'The dry, airless conditions down there have more or less mummified it,' Rayner said. 'Once we get it out it shouldn't be too difficult to identify.'

Rayner went over to the nearest phone and pressed 999. Mum and I watched in silence as he asked for the police.

'Hello? This is Rayner Alten from the BFC Power plant on the Preston Way. We just discovered a body in one of our underground pipes . . . Yes, that's right . . . Yes . . . No, it's on one of our monitors. That's right . . . OK.' Rayner put down the phone. 'They're sending someone right over.'

The door to the Operating Room opened, making us all jump. Dad walked in, only to stop in his tracks when he saw all our faces.

'What's the matter?'

'Oh, Jack, look!' Mum said, distressed. 'Look what VIMS found.'

Jack walked slowly into the room and up to the monitor. He stared and stared at it, never turning his head.

'How did that woman get down there?' I asked.

'I can only think that she was put in the pipes the day before they were sealed and covered over. That means it had to be someone who worked here at BFC or some-one who worked for the construction company. It had to be someone who knew the construction schedule,' Rayner mused.

'Or it might've been someone who dumped the body there and then was just lucky,' I said.

'Well, there's no point in speculating. The police will be here soon and then I'll turn the whole matter over to them.'

A body. I still couldn't believe it. An Antarctic chill went trickling down my back.

'Jack . . .'

The note of horror and intense pain in Mum's voice had my head whipping round. Mum and Jack were looking at each other. Mum had tears trickling down her face and Jack looked so, so sad. They regarded each other as if they were the last two people in the world. The rest of us had ceased to exist.

'Tell me I'm wrong,' Mum begged.

Jack didn't answer.

'Jack, please tell me I'm wrong.'

Frowning, I tried to work out what was going on.

'It's Alison, isn't it?' Mum's voice was the merest whisper.

'Who's Alison?' I asked. And then it clicked. 'You mean Alison, Dad's first wife?'

Dad didn't take his eyes off Mum.

'Shall I get VIMS to turn over the body so we can see her face?' Mum whispered.

Dad shook his head. 'It's her. It's Alison's body down there in the pipe.'

'Oh, Jack . . .'

'Carol, I didn't kill her. I mean, I didn't murder her. It was an accident. I was up on the scaffold tower working late. She came up to see me and we started arguing. That was all we ever did. I didn't want another hateful, hurtful argument and I told her so. I told her I wanted a divorce and she flew at me. She started punching and slapping and I lost my temper and pushed her.' Jack buried his head in his hands. 'I didn't hit her, I swear. I just pushed her. She staggered backwards and fell off the scaffolding. By the time I'd got down to the ground, she was dead and I . . . I just panicked.'

'So you hid her body down in the pipes, knowing they were due to be sealed the following day,' said Rayner. 'And all this time you got away with it.'

'Got away with it? I don't think so,' Dad said bitterly. 'If you'd had my nightmares over the last eight years, then you wouldn't accuse me of getting away with anything.'

'But that can't be Alison.' What were they all talking

about? Everyone had gone mad except me. 'Alison is living in Australia. You said so.'

Only then did Dad turn to me. He didn't say anything. He didn't have to. It was all in his eyes.

'I don't understand.' The words were a shocked whisper. 'Why wasn't the body found years ago, even after the pipes had been sealed?'

'We only started using the mechanical pigs a month ago,' Rayner said slowly. He was working it out as he spoke. 'The pigs in this section of the pipes must've repeatedly disturbed the body. That's why they kept reporting problems, because Alison's body was causing an obstruction.'

'That's why you didn't want me to let Rayner use VIMS,' Mum realized. 'You knew what the problem here was all along.'

Jack bowed his head, no longer able to look at Mum.

'Jack, was it you who sabotaged VIMS to make sure Rayner wouldn't get it?' Mum asked quietly.

'Yes. The two of us . . .' He looked at me. 'The three of us were happy. I was desperate to make sure nothing changed that. I care about the two of you very much.'

'But VIMS knocked Mum off the stage,' I flared at him. 'If you care so much about Mum, how could you let VIMS do that?'

And in that moment, I almost hated him.

'Dominic, that was never meant to happen. You have

to believe me. I swear VIMS was never meant to hurt anyone – especially not Carol. I changed VIMS' software so that he'd fail the demo to the suits and uniforms. It was the only way I could make sure that he wasn't lent to Rayner. I wanted to get rid of all the changes I'd made to VIMS' system, but your mum locked everyone out so I no longer had access to his programming,' Jack said, anguished. 'I couldn't change the software back in time. I never, ever wanted him to hurt Carol.'

But VIMS *had* hurt Mum. And all because Jack was so busy trying to hide what he'd done in the past that he didn't think about the consequences of what he was doing in the present. Each lie had led to another. Every attempt to hide the truth had backfired. Jack wasn't going to get off that easily.

'Mum's accident was still your fault. You're the one who . . . who . . .' I stared at Jack as something else occurred to me. 'It was *you*. You were the one who sent VIMS after me last night.'

'What's this?' Mum asked, startled.

'That's why VIMS was in our house, Mum,' I told her. 'He crashed through the window in your work room and came after me.'

'You sent VIMS after my son?'

'I . . .'

Mum flew out of her chair. 'YOU SENT VIMS AFTER DOMINIC?'

165

'I think I went a little mad.' Jack groaned. 'I changed his programming from Julie's account at Desica. It only took me a couple of minutes to come to my senses, but by then Dominic had used his VIMS password to lock me out. I couldn't delete the command. So I drove like a demon to get to the house before VIMS did.'

'You tried to hurt my son?' said Mum, appalled, her eyes aflame.

Jack shook his head but he didn't say a word. He couldn't. Mum's expression began to set as she stared at Jack. Strangely enough, in that moment, my own anger dropped away.

'No, Mum,' I said slowly. 'Dad saved my life. He made VIMS come after him instead. He saved my life.'

'Jack, where were you this morning?' Mum asked.

'At Desica,' Jack replied.

'Still trying to cover your tracks.' It wasn't a question.

Mum and Jack regarded each other. It's strange to think you can have a deathly hush in a machine room full of noise, but we did. No one spoke for a good few minutes. Finally Jack looked down at the ground. Mum didn't take her eyes off him. I couldn't figure out what she was thinking. Her face was a mask.

'What happens now?' Jack asked at last.

'Couldn't we . . . somehow . . .' I began.

'I've already called the police,' Rayner reminded us all. 'They'll be here any moment.'

166

'Then it's over.' Jack sighed. His whole body slumped as he put his head in his hands.

Mum walked over to him and took his hands away from his face. Jack's hands dropped to his side. Mum looked into his eyes as if searching for something and Jack didn't look away, although it looked as if it took all his will power not to do so.

'Oh, Jack . . .' Mum whispered.

'I . . .'

Mum shook her head, interrupting him. 'Don't say anything.'

Jack's lips clamped together. Then Mum took Jack's hands in her own, and a moment later they were hugging each other tight. I walked over to Mum and . . . and Dad and they both hugged me too.

And behind us, I heard the door open. The police had arrived.

Chapter Twenty

Endings and Beginnings

So that's pretty much it really. The police arrested Dad and formally charged him. Mum and I were taken to the police station as well. Rayner told us later that with VIMS' help, Alison's body was brought to the surface. I kept thinking, hoping, *praying* that it was all a mistake, a misunderstanding. I think a part of me really believed that, until VIMS brought Alison's body to the surface. Then there could be no doubt.

And after that it's just a kaleidoscope of images. Faces, mainly. The police, Liam, my teacher, Pops, even some reporters who tried to get an interview. I didn't realize it at the time, but initially, the police thought Mum was somehow involved in Alison's death. Mum had to go down to the police station over and over again to make statement after statement. And I didn't get to see Jack until the trial. That was one of the worst things about the whole business.

The trial was horrible. The prosecutor kept trying to

persuade the jury that Dad was guilty of murder not manslaughter. He kept bringing in the fact that Dad had sent VIMS after me. I think the fact that Mum and I stuck by him, plus the fact that he saved my life, managed to convince them that Dad wasn't a murderer. When the jury came back into the court after retiring to consider their verdict, it felt like my heart was revving up until it must surely take off out of my body. I crossed my fingers, willing the foreman to say the right thing.

'On the charge of murder, do you, the jury, find the defendant, Jack Brickhill, guilty or not guilty?'

'Not guilty.'

My heart stopped. My breathing stopped. I crossed my fingers tighter.

'On the charge of manslaughter, do you, the jury, find the defendant, Jack Brickhill, guilty or not guilty?'

The foreman seemed to take for ever to answer. But at last his answer came.

'Guilty.'

'No . . .' The whisper came out of me in a rush. They couldn't find Jack guilty. It was an accident. He told them it was an accident. How could they find him guilty? 'Mum . . .'

'Shush.'

We listened to the judge sum up. He spouted on about how even though the jury had found the death of Alison Brickhill to be an accident and involuntary manslaughter, the fact that Jack had covered it up for all these years did not help his case. Pops put his arm around my shoulder. I didn't realize why until tears splashed onto my hands lying in my lap.

The judge sentenced Jack to five years in prison.

And as Jack was being led away, he looked up at us. I wasn't the only one crying. Mum wiped her eyes with the back of her hand. We left the court room in a daze. D'you know, I don't remember the next couple of days after that, I really don't. I think my mind just switched off or shut down or something. I just kept re-living the whole last day in court, over and over.

And blaming myself. Blaming myself for sneaking into Desica for a glimpse at VIMS. Blaming myself for not leaving well enough alone and forcing Jack into thinking he had to get rid of me. Blaming myself for asking Rayner if I could bring VIMS to his power plant.

With Mum's help and a lot of time, I now realize that it was Dad's actions, not mine, that had led to their inevitable conclusion. I didn't really believe that. Not really. Not until Mum showed me one of the letters Dad had written to her.

Dearest Carol,

I don't know what to write, what to say to you and Dominic. I've let both of you down so badly. I want you

to know, you can't hate me any more than I hate myself.
I keep looking back to that night and wondering what I
could and should've done differently. There has to be
something. I should've gone down to the ground to meet
Alison, instead of insisting that she came up to me. I
could've picked a better time to tell her that I wanted a
divorce, instead of just blurting it out in a fit of temper.

I'm not making excuses. All these years I've been
living half a life. I've always known that somewhere,
somehow, my past would catch up with me. It's just the
bitter timing that I resent. Does Dominic hate me? I
hope not. I made a dreadful, dreadful mistake, then
made things worse by not facing up to what I'd done. I
hope that some day you and Dominic can find it in your
hearts to forgive me. I know this is asking a lot but I
need to know where I stand with you.

Will you wait for me? Can we carry on from where
we left off when I come out of prison, with no more
secrets between us? Do you still love me? You can write
back with just one word. Yes or no. If it's no, I'll
understand.

All my love for ever,
Jack.

'What did you write back and tell him?' I asked.
'I haven't written back yet,' said Mum.

'Are you going to?'

At first, I thought that Mum wasn't going to answer me. 'I have to give him an answer – one way or another.'

'What will your answer be?' I asked.

'What d'you think it should be?'

'You still love him, don't you?'

Silence stretched out between us like boundless elastic.

'Yes,' Mum said at last.

'Well,' I said carefully. 'There's your answer then.'

Mum took the letter out of my hands and stared at it for several moments. Then she walked into her bedroom, closing the door behind her.

I've had a lot of time to think, over the year that Dad's been in prison. Why do I still call him Dad? Because that's how I think of him – in spite of everything that's happened. He's still my dad. VIMS was an 'it', then a 'him', then an 'it' again. But it doesn't work that way with people. It doesn't work that way when thoughts and feelings and hopes and fears come into the picture – and maybe that's just as well.

Mum and I are hoping that Dad will be out of prison in another two years, with time off for good behaviour. And as soon as he comes out, he and Mum are planning to get married straight away. I can't wait. We visit Dad once a month but it's not enough. Not really. I miss him every day. But however much I miss him, I know Mum misses him more. Sometimes, in the early hours of the morning, when the house is still, I can hear Mum crying. I want to go to her and tell her everything will be OK. That Dad will be out soon. But I know that that would just make her feel worse. So I lie in my bed, waiting for her to stop crying so that I can then drift off back to sleep.

And what has this whole thing taught me? Well, for a start I now realize that sometimes things just happen and there's nothing you can do about it. I've stopped beating myself up over the fact that Matt Viner is no longer my friend. That's just the way it is. And I've stopped wasting my days thinking, What if . . .? and, If only . . . I don't blame myself any more – well, not all the time at any rate. So that's progress.

Mum asked to be transferred onto another project and Desica were more than happy to oblige. When VIMS finally went live – which it did two months ago – Julie Resnick got all the publicity and the credit. But VIMS is – was – my mum's idea, my mum's creation. But Mum wanted nothing more to do with it after Dad went to prison. So I guess if Mum doesn't mind about Julie getting all the glory, then neither should I.

Did I mention, Liam has been terrific? I thought that maybe he'd prefer not to talk to me or something, or maybe he'd be too embarrassed, but he's been one hundred per cent beside me. In fact most people have been really kind about it. Matt Vinyl wasn't, but then I never expected anything else. He still tries to push me around, but less frequently these days. I think it's because I'm not scared of him any more. Do you want to hear something strange? It was only when I realized that I was no longer scared of him that I realized why I had been scared of him in the past. I wasn't scared that he'd duff me up or anything like that. But I was scared because he wasn't my friend any more. Scared because I didn't know why. Scared because I was blaming my limp and my mum for being a bit famous and a whole load of other nonsense reasons. It wasn't my fault – at least not all my fault. All Matt had to say was, 'Dominic, stop going on about your mum.' And I would've shut up. They say that if you show fear to a dog they can sense it. But if you are fearless then most of the time they'll back down. I think it's a bit like that with me and Matt. We'll never be friends again – but that's just the way it is. Onwards and upwards.

Dad will be out of prison soon. Whenever I feel a bit down, I just hold onto that thought. Dad will be out of prison soon and we'll all be together for ever. And we'll be a real family. How do I know all that? Easy. Because we've survived this far and we still all care about each other. So if we can make it through all these bad times, how can there be anything left but good times ahead?

About the author

MALORIE BLACKMAN is acknowledged as one of today's most imaginative and convincing writers for young readers. *Noughts & Crosses* has won several prizes, including the Children's Book Award. Malorie is also the only author to have won the Young Telegraph/ Gimme 5 Award twice with *Hacker* and *Thief!* Her work has appeared on screen, with *Pig-Heart Boy*, which was shortlisted for the Carnegie Medal, being adapted into a BAFTA-award-winning TV serial. Malorie has also written a number of titles for younger readers.

In 2005, Malorie was honoured with the Eleanor Farjeon Award in recognition of her distinguished contribution to the world of children's books.

In 2008, she received an OBE for her services to children's literature.

www.**malorieblackman**.co.uk